The Pelican Shakespeare
General Editors

STEPHEN ORGEL
A. R. BRAUNMULLER

written:
1604–1605
published:
1623

setting: 8th century BC

King Lear
A Conflated Text

themes: justice, authority vs. chaos
reconciliation
motifs: madness, betrayal
symbols: storm, blindness,
wheel of fortune

Sir Henry Irving as King Lear, 1892
(Drawing by J. Bernard Partridge)

William Shakespeare

King Lear

A Conflated Text

EDITED BY STEPHEN ORGEL

PENGUIN BOOKS

PENGUIN BOOKS

Published by the Penguin Group

Penguin Group (USA) Inc., 375 Hudson Street, New York, New York 10014, U.S.A.

Penguin Group (Canada), 90 Eglinton Avenue East, Suite 700, Toronto, Ontario,
Canada M4P 2Y3 (a division of Pearson Penguin Canada Inc.)

Penguin Books Ltd, 80 Strand, London WC2R 0RL, England

Penguin Ireland, 25 St Stephen's Green, Dublin 2, Ireland (a division of Penguin Books Ltd)

Penguin Group (Australia), 250 Camberwell Road, Camberwell,
Victoria 3124, Australia (a division of Pearson Australia Group Pty Ltd)

Penguin Books India Pvt Ltd, 11 Community Centre, Panchsheel Park,
New Delhi – 110 017, India

Penguin Group (NZ), 67 Apollo Drive, Rosedale, North Shore 0632, New Zealand
(a division of Pearson New Zealand Ltd)

Penguin Books (South Africa) (Pty) Ltd, 24 Sturdee Avenue, Rosebank,
Johannesburg 2196, South Africa

Penguin Books Ltd, Registered Offices: 80 Strand, London WC2R 0RL, England

The Tragedy of King Lear edited by Alfred Harbage published in
the United States of America in Penguin Books 1958
Revised edition published 1970
This new edition edited by Stephen Orgel published 1999

21 23 25 24 22

Copyright © Penguin Books Inc., 1958, 1970
Copyright © Penguin Putnam Inc., 1999
All rights reserved

ISBN 978-0-14-071476-0

Printed in the United States of America
Set in Garamond
Designed by Virginia Norey

Contents

Publisher's Note

IT IS ALMOST half a century since the first volumes of the Pelican Shakespeare appeared under the general editorship of Alfred Harbage. The fact that a new edition, rather than simply a revision, has been undertaken reflects the profound changes textual and critical studies of Shakespeare have undergone in the past twenty years. For the new Pelican series, the texts of the plays and poems have been thoroughly revised in accordance with recent scholarship, and in some cases have been entirely reedited. New introductions and notes have been provided in all the volumes. But the new Shakespeare is also designed as a successor to the original series; the previous editions have been taken into account, and the advice of the previous editors has been solicited where it was feasible to do so.

Certain textual features of the new Pelican Shakespeare should be particularly noted. All lines are numbered that contain a word, phrase, or allusion explained in the glossarial notes. In addition, for convenience, every tenth line is also numbered, in italics when no annotation is indicated. The intrusive and often inaccurate place headings inserted by early editors are omitted (as is becoming standard practice), but for the convenience of those who miss them, an indication of locale now appears as the first item in the annotation of each scene.

In the interest of both elegance and utility, each speech prefix is set in a separate line when the speaker's lines are in verse, except when those words form the second half of a verse line. Thus the verse form of the speech is kept visually intact. What is printed as verse and what is printed as prose has, in general, the authority of the original texts. Departures from the original texts in this regard have only the authority of editorial tradition and the judgment of the Pelican editors; and, in a few instances, are admittedly arbitrary.

The Theatrical World

Economic realities determined the theatrical world in which Shakespeare's plays were written, performed, and received. For centuries in England, the primary theatrical tradition was nonprofessional. Craft guilds (or "mysteries") provided religious drama – mystery plays – as part of the celebration of religious and civic festivals, and schools and universities staged classical and neoclassical drama in both Latin and English as part of their curricula. In these forms, drama was established and socially acceptable. Professional theater, in contrast, existed on the margins of society. The acting companies were itinerant; playhouses could be any available space – the great halls of the aristocracy, town squares, civic halls, inn yards, fair booths, or open fields – and income was sporadic, dependent on the passing of the hat or on the bounty of local patrons. The actors, moreover, were considered little better than vagabonds, constantly in danger of arrest or expulsion.

In the late 1560s and 1570s, however, English professional theater began to gain respectability. Wealthy aristocrats fond of drama – the Lord Admiral, for example, or the Lord Chamberlain – took acting companies under their protection so that the players technically became members of their households and were no longer subject to arrest as homeless or masterless men. Permanent theaters were first built at this time as well, allowing the companies to control and charge for entry to their performances.

Shakespeare's livelihood, and the stunning artistic explosion in which he participated, depended on pragmatic and architectural effort. Professional theater requires ways to restrict access to its offerings; if it does not, and admission fees cannot be charged, the actors do not get paid, the costumes go to a pawnbroker, and there is no such thing as a professional, ongoing theatrical tradition. The answer to that economic need arrived in the late 1560s and 1570s with the creation of the so-called public or amphitheater playhouse. Recent discoveries indicate that the precursor of the Globe playhouse in London (where Shakespeare's mature plays were presented) and the Rose theater (which presented Christopher Marlowe's plays and some of Shakespeare's earliest ones) was the Red Lion theater of 1567. Archaeological studies of the foundations of the Rose and Globe theaters have revealed that the open-air theater of the 1590s and later was probably a polygonal building with fourteen to twenty or twenty-four sides, multistoried, from 75 to 100 feet in diameter, with a raised, partly covered "thrust" stage that projected into a group of standing patrons, or "groundlings," and a covered gallery, seating up to 2,500 or more (very crowded) spectators.

These theaters might have been about half full on any given day, though the audiences were larger on holidays or when a play was advertised, as old and new were, through printed playbills posted around London. The metropolitan area's late-Tudor, early-Stuart population (circa 1590–1620) has been estimated at about 150,000 to 250,000. It has been supposed that in the mid-1590s there were about 15,000 spectators per week at the public theaters; thus, as many as 10 percent of the local population went to the theater regularly. Consequently, the theaters' repertories – the plays available for this experienced and frequent audience – had to change often: in the month between September 15 and October 15, 1595, for instance, the Lord Admiral's Men performed twenty-eight times in eighteen different plays.

Since natural light illuminated the amphitheaters' stages, performances began between noon and two o'clock and ran without a break for two or three hours. They often concluded with a jig, a fencing display, or some other nondramatic exhibition. Weather conditions determined the season for the amphitheaters: plays were performed every day (including Sundays, sometimes, to clerical dismay) except during Lent – the forty days before Easter – or periods of plague, or sometimes during the summer months when law courts were not in session and the most affluent members of the audience were not in London.

To a modern theatergoer, an amphitheater stage like that of the Rose or Globe would appear an unfamiliar mixture of plainness and elaborate decoration. Much of the structure was carved or painted, sometimes to imitate marble; elsewhere, as under the canopy projecting over the stage, to represent the stars and the zodiac. Appropriate painted canvas pictures (of Jerusalem, for example, if the play was set in that city) were apparently hung on the wall behind the acting area, and tragedies were accompanied by black hangings, presumably something like crepe festoons or bunting. Although these theaters did not employ what we would call scenery, early modern spectators saw numerous large props, such as the "bar" at which a prisoner stood during a trial, the "mossy bank" where lovers reclined, an arbor for amorous conversation, a chariot, gallows, tables, trees, beds, thrones, writing desks, and so forth. Audiences might learn a scene's location from a sign (reading "Athens," for example) carried across the stage (as in Bertolt Brecht's twentieth-century productions). Equally captivating (and equally irritating to the theater's enemies) were the rich costumes and personal props the actors used: the most valuable items in the surviving theatrical inventories are the swords, gowns, robes, crowns, and other items worn or carried by the performers.

Magic appealed to Shakespeare's audiences as much as it does to us today, and the theater exploited many deceptive and spectacular devices. A winch in the loft above the stage, called "the heavens," could lower and raise actors

playing gods, goddesses, and other supernatural figures to
and from the main acting area, just as one or more trap-
doors permitted entrances and exits to and from the area,
called "hell," beneath the stage. Actors wore elementary
makeup such as wigs, false beards, and face paint, and
they employed pig's bladders filled with animal blood to
make wounds seem more real. They had rudimentary but
effective ways of pretending to behead or hang a person.
Supernumeraries (stagehands or actors not needed in a
particular scene) could make thunder sounds (by shaking
a metal sheet or rolling an iron ball down a chute) and
show lightning (by blowing inflammable resin through
tubes into a flame). Elaborate fireworks enhanced the effects of dragons flying through the air or imitated such ce-
lestial phenomena as comets, shooting stars, and multiple
suns. Horses' hoofbeats, bells (located perhaps in the
tower above the stage), trumpets and drums, clocks, can-
non shots and gunshots, and the like were common
sound effects. And the music of viols, cornets, oboes, and
recorders was a regular feature of theatrical performances.

For two relatively brief spans, from the late 1570s to
1590 and from 1599 to 1614, the amphitheaters com-
peted with the so-called private, or indoor, theaters,
which originated as, or later represented themselves as,
educational institutions training boys as singers for
church services and court performances. These indoor
theaters had two features that were distinct from the amphitheaters': their personnel and their playing spaces. The
amphitheaters' adult companies included both adult
men, who played the male roles, and boys, who played the
female roles; the private, or indoor, theater companies, on
the other hand, were entirely composed of boys aged
about 8 to 16, who were, or could pretend to be, candidates for singers in a church or a royal boys' choir.
(Until 1660, professional theatrical companies included
no women.) The playing space would appear much more
familiar to modern audiences than the long-vanished

amphitheaters; the later indoor theaters were, in fact, the ancestors of the typical modern theater. They were enclosed spaces, usually rectangular, with the stage filling one end of the rectangle and the audience arrayed in seats or benches across (and sometimes lining) the building's longer axis. These spaces staged plays less frequently than the public theaters (perhaps only once a week) and held far fewer spectators than the amphitheaters: about 200 to 600, as opposed to 2,500 or more. Fewer patrons mean a smaller gross income, unless each pays more. Not surprisingly, then, private theaters charged higher prices than the amphitheaters, probably sixpence, as opposed to a penny for the cheapest entry.

Protected from the weather, the indoor theaters presented plays later in the day than the amphitheaters, and used artificial illumination – candles in sconces or candelabra. But candles melt, and need replacing, snuffing, and trimming, and these practical requirements may have been part of the reason the indoor theaters introduced breaks in the performance, the intermission so dear to the heart of theatergoers and to the pocketbooks of theater concessionaires ever since. Whether motivated by the need to tend to the candles or by the entrepreneurs' wishing to sell oranges and liquor, or both, the indoor theaters eventually established the modern convention of the noncontinuous performance. In the early modern "private" theater, musical performances apparently filled the intermissions, which in Stuart theater jargon seem to have been called "acts."

At the end of the first decade of the seventeenth century, the distinction between public amphitheaters and private indoor companies ceased. For various cultural, political, and economic reasons, individual companies gained control of both the public, open-air theaters and the indoor ones, and companies mixing adult men and boys took over the formerly "private" theaters. Despite the death of the boys' companies and of their highly innovative theaters (for which such luminous playwrights as Ben Jonson, George Chapman, and John Marston wrote), their playing spaces and conventions had an immense impact on subsequent plays: not merely for the intervals (which stressed the artistic and architectonic importance of "acts"), but also because they introduced political and social satire as a popular dramatic ingredient, even in tragedy, and a wider range of actorly effects, encouraged by their more intimate playing spaces.

Even the briefest sketch of the Shakespearean theatrical world would be incomplete without some comment on the social and cultural dimensions of theaters and playing in the period. In an intensely hierarchical and status-conscious society, professional actors and their ventures had hardly any respectability; as we have indicated, to protect themselves against laws designed to curb vagabondage and the increase of masterless men, actors resorted to the near-fiction that they were the servants of noble masters, and wore their distinctive livery. Hence the company for which Shakespeare wrote in the 1590s called itself the Lord Chamberlain's Men and pretended that the public, money-getting performances were in fact rehearsals for private performances before that high court official. From 1598, the Privy Council had licensed theatrical companies, and after 1603, with the accession of King James I, the companies gained explicit royal protection, just as the Queen's Men had for a time under Queen Elizabeth. The Chamberlain's Men became the King's Men, and the other companies were patronized by the other members of the royal family.

These designations were legal fictions that half-concealed an important economic and social development, the evolution away from the theater's organization on the model of the guild, a self-regulating confraternity of individual artisans, into a proto-capitalist organization. Shakespeare's company became a joint-stock company, where persons who supplied capital and, in some cases,

such as Shakespeare's, capital and talent, employed themselves and others in earning a return on that capital. This
development meant that actors and theater companies
were outside both the traditional guild structures, which
required some form of civic or royal charter, and the feu-
dal household organization of master-and-servant. This
anomalous, maverick social and economic condition
made theater companies practically unruly and poten-
tially even dangerous; consequently, numerous official
bodies – including the London metropolitan and ecclesi-
astical authorities as well as, occasionally, the royal court
itself – tried, without much success, to control and even
to disband them.

Public officials had good reason to want to close the
theaters: they were attractive nuisances – they drew often
riotous crowds, they were always noisy, and they could be
politically offensive and socially insubordinate. Until the
Civil War, however, anti-theatrical forces failed to shut
down professional theater, for many reasons – limited
surveillance and few police powers, tensions or outright
hostilities among the agencies that sought to check or
channel theatrical activity, and lack of clear policies for
control. Another reason must have been the theaters' un-
deniable popularity. Curtailing any activity enjoyed by
such a substantial percentage of the population was diffi-
cult, as various Roman emperors attempting to limit cir-
cuses had learned, and the Tudor-Stuart audience was not
merely large, it was socially diverse and included women.
The prevalence of public entertainment in this period
has been underestimated. In fact, fairs, holidays, games,
sporting events, the equivalent of modern parades, freak
shows, and street exhibitions all abounded, but the theater was the most widely and frequently available entertainment to which people of every class had access. That
fact helps account both for its quantity and for the fear
and anger it aroused.

WILLIAM SHAKESPEARE OF
STRATFORD-UPON-AVON, GENTLEMAN

Many people have said that we know very little about William Shakespeare's life – pinheads and postcards are often mentioned as appropriately tiny surfaces on which to record the available information. More imaginatively and perhaps more correctly, Ralph Waldo Emerson wrote, "Shakespeare is the only biographer of Shakespeare. . . . So far from Shakespeare's being the least known, he is the one person in all modern history fully known to us."

In fact, we know more about Shakespeare's life than we do about almost any other English writer's of his era. His last will and testament (dated March 25, 1616) survives, as do numerous legal contracts and court documents involving Shakespeare as principal or witness, and parish records in Stratford and London. Shakespeare appears quite often in official records of King James's royal court, and of course Shakespeare's name appears on numerous title pages and in the written and recorded words of his literary contemporaries Robert Greene, Henry Chettle, Francis Meres, John Davies of Hereford, Ben Jonson, and many others. Indeed, if we make due allowance for the bloating of modern, run-of-the-mill bureaucratic records, more information has survived over the past four hundred years about William Shakespeare of Stratford-upon-Avon, Warwickshire, than is likely to survive in the next four hundred years about any reader of these words.

What we do not have are entire categories of information – Shakespeare's private letters or diaries, drafts and revisions of poems and plays, critical prefaces or essays, commendatory verse for other writers' works, or instructions guiding his fellow actors in their performances, for instance – that we imagine would help us understand and appreciate his surviving writings. For all we know, many such data never existed as written records. Many literary and theatrical critics, not knowing what might once have existed, more or less cheerfully accept the situation; some even make a theoretical virtue of it by claiming that such data are irrelevant to understanding and interpreting the plays and poems.

So, what do we know about William Shakespeare, the man responsible for thirty-seven or perhaps more plays, more than 150 sonnets, two lengthy narrative poems, and some shorter poems?

While many families by the name of Shakespeare (or some variant spelling) can be identified in the English Midlands as far back as the twelfth century, it seems likely that the dramatist's grandfather, Richard, moved to Snitterfield, a town not far from Stratford-upon-Avon, sometime before 1529. In Snitterfield, Richard Shakespeare leased farmland from the very wealthy Robert Arden. By 1552, Richard's son John had moved to a large house on Henley Street in Stratford-upon-Avon, the house that stands today as "The Birthplace." In Stratford, John Shakespeare traded as a glover, dealt in wool, and lent money at interest; he also served in a variety of civic posts, including "High Bailiff," the municipality's equivalent of mayor. In 1557, he married Robert Arden's youngest daughter, Mary. Mary and John had four sons – William was the oldest – and four daughters, of whom only Joan outlived her most celebrated sibling. William was baptized (an event entered in the Stratford parish church records) on April 26, 1564, and it has become customary, without any good factual support, to suppose he was born on April 23, which happens to be the feast day of Saint George, patron saint of England, and is also the date on which he died, in 1616. Shakespeare married Anne Hathaway in 1582, when he was eighteen and she was twenty-six; their first child was born five months later. It has been generally assumed that the marriage was enforced and subsequently unhappy, but these are only assumptions; it has been estimated, for instance, that up to one third of Elizabethan brides were pregnant when they married. Anne and William Shakespeare had three children: Susanna, who married a prominent local physician, John Hall; and the twins Hamnet, who died young in 1596, and Judith, who married Thomas Quiney – apparently a rather shady individual. The name Hamnet was unusual but not unique: he and his twin sister were named for their godparents, Shakespeare's neighbors Hamnet and Judith Sadler. Shakespeare's father died in 1601 (the year of *Hamlet*), and Mary Arden Shakespeare died in 1608 (the year of *Coriolanus*). William Shakespeare's last surviving direct descendant was his granddaughter Elizabeth Hall, who died in 1670.

Between the birth of the twins in 1585 and a clear reference to Shakespeare as a practicing London dramatist in Robert Greene's sensationalizing, satiric pamphlet, *Greene's Groatsworth of Wit* (1592), there is no record of where William Shakespeare was or what he was doing. These seven so-called lost years have been imaginatively filled by scholars and other students of Shakespeare: some think he traveled to Italy, or fought in the Low Countries, or studied law or medicine, or worked as an apprentice actor/writer, and so on to even more fanciful possibilities. Whatever the biographical facts for those "lost" years, Greene's nasty remarks in 1592 testify to professional envy and to the fact that Shakespeare already had a successful career in London. Speaking to his fellow playwrights, Greene warns both generally and specifically:

> . . . trust them [actors] not: for there is an upstart crow, beautified with our feathers, that with his tiger's heart wrapped in a player's hide supposes he is as well able to bombast out a blank verse as the best of you; and being an absolute Johannes Factotum, is in his own conceit the only Shake-scene in a country.

The passage mimics a line from *3 Henry VI* (hence the play must have been performed before Greene wrote) and seems to say that "Shake-scene" is both actor and playwright, a jack-of-all-trades. That same year, Henry Chettle protested Greene's remarks in *Kind-Heart's Dream,* and each of the next two years saw the publication of poems – *Venus and Adonis* and *The Rape of Lucrece,* respectively – publicly ascribed to (and dedicated by) Shakespeare. Early in 1595 he was named one of the senior members of a prominent acting company, the Lord Chamberlain's Men, when they received payment for court performances during the 1594 Christmas season.

Clearly, Shakespeare had achieved both success and reputation in London. In 1596, upon Shakespeare's application, the College of Arms granted his father the now-familiar coat of arms he had taken the first steps to obtain almost twenty years before, and in 1598, John's son – now permitted to call himself "gentleman" – took a 10 percent share in the new Globe playhouse. In 1597, he bought a substantial bourgeois house, called New Place, in Stratford – the garden remains, but Shakespeare's house, several times rebuilt, was torn down in 1759 – and over the next few years Shakespeare spent large sums buying land and making other investments in the town and its environs. Though he worked in London, his family remained in Stratford, and he seems always to have considered Stratford the home he would eventually return to. Something approaching a disinterested appreciation of Shakespeare's popular and professional status appears in Francis Meres's *Palladis Tamia* (1598), a not especially imaginative and perhaps therefore persuasive record of literary reputations. Reviewing contemporary English writers, Meres lists the titles of many of Shakespeare's plays, including one not now known, *Love's Labor's Won,* and praises his "mellifluous & hony-tongued" "sugred Sonnets," which were then circulating in manuscript (they were first collected in 1609). Meres describes Shakespeare as "one of the best" English playwrights of both comedy and tragedy. In *Remains . . . Concerning Britain* (1605),

William Camden – a more authoritative source than the imitative Meres – calls Shakespeare one of the "most pregnant witts of these our times" and joins him with such writers as Chapman, Daniel, Jonson, Marston, and Spenser. During the first decades of the seventeenth century, publishers began to attribute numerous play quartos, including some non-Shakespearean ones, to Shakespeare, either by name or initials, and we may assume that they deemed Shakespeare's name and supposed authorship, true or false, commercially attractive.

For the next ten years or so, various records show Shakespeare's dual career as playwright and man of the theater in London, and as an important local figure in Stratford. In 1608-9 his acting company – designated the "King's Men" soon after King James had succeeded Queen Elizabeth in 1603 – rented, refurbished, and opened a small interior playing space, the Blackfriars theater, in London, and Shakespeare was once again listed as a substantial sharer in the group of proprietors of the playhouse. By May 11, 1612, however, he describes himself as a Stratford resident in a London lawsuit – an indication that he had withdrawn from day-to-day professional activity and returned to the town where he had always had his main financial interests. When Shakespeare bought a substantial residential building in London, the Blackfriars Gatehouse, close to the theater of the same name, on March 10, 1613, he is recorded as William Shakespeare "of Stratford upon Avon in the county of Warwick, gentleman," and he named several London residents as the building's trustees. Still, he continued to participate in theatrical activity: when the new Earl of Rutland needed an allegorical design to bear as a shield, or *impresa,* at the celebration of King James's Accession Day, March 24, 1613, the earl's accountant recorded a payment of 44 shillings to Shakespeare for the device with its motto.

For the last few years of his life, Shakespeare evidently

concentrated his activities in the town of his birth. Most of the final records concern business transactions in Stratford, ending with the notation of his death on April 23, 1616, and burial in Holy Trinity Church, Stratford-upon-Avon.

THE QUESTION OF AUTHORSHIP

The history of ascribing Shakespeare's plays (the poems do not come up so often) to someone else began, as it continues, peculiarly. The earliest published claim that someone else wrote Shakespeare's plays appeared in an 1856 article by Delia Bacon in the American journal *Putnam's Monthly* – although an Englishman, Thomas Wilmot, had shared his doubts in private (even secretive) conversations with friends near the end of the eighteenth century. Bacon's was a sad personal history that ended in madness and poverty, but the year after her article, she published, with great difficulty and the bemused assistance of Nathaniel Hawthorne (then United States Consul in Liverpool, England), her *Philosophy of the Plays of Shakspere Unfolded.* This huge, ornately written, confusing farrago is almost unreadable; sometimes its intents, to say nothing of its arguments, disappear entirely beneath near-raving, ecstatic writing. Tumbled in with much supposed "philosophy" appear the claims that Francis Bacon (from whom Delia Bacon eventually claimed descent), Walter Ralegh, and several other contemporaries of Shakespeare's had written the plays. The book had little impact except as a ridiculed curiosity.

Once proposed, however, the issue gained momentum among people whose conviction was the greater in proportion to their ignorance of sixteenth- and seventeenth-century English literature, history, and society. Another American amateur, Catherine P. Ashmead Windle, made the next influential contribution to the cause when she published *Report to the British Museum* (1882), wherein she promised to open "the Cipher of Francis Bacon," though what she mostly offers, in the words of S. Schoenbaum, is "demented allegorizing." An entire new cottage industry grew from Windle's suggestion that the texts contain hidden, cryptographically discoverable ciphers – "clues" – to their authorship; and today there are not only books devoted to the putative ciphers, but also pamphlets, journals, and newsletters.

Although Baconians have led the pack of those seeking a substitute Shakespeare, in *"Shakespeare" Identified* (1920), J. Thomas Looney became the first published "Oxfordian" when he proposed Edward de Vere, seventeenth earl of Oxford, as the secret author of Shakespeare's plays. Also for Oxford and his "authorship" there are today dedicated societies, articles, journals, and books. Less popular candidates – Queen Elizabeth and Christopher Marlowe among them – have had adherents, but the movement seems to have divided into two main contending factions, Baconian and Oxfordian. (For further details on all the candidates for "Shakespeare," see S. Schoenbaum, *Shakespeare's Lives,* 2nd ed., 1991.)

The Baconians, the Oxfordians, and supporters of other candidates have one trait in common – they are snobs. Every pro-Bacon or pro-Oxford tract sooner or later claims that the historical William Shakespeare of Stratford-upon-Avon could not have written the plays because he could not have had the training, the university education, the experience, and indeed the imagination or background their author supposedly possessed. Only a learned genius like Bacon or an aristocrat like Oxford could have written such fine plays. (As it happens, lucky male children of the middle class had access to better education than most aristocrats in Elizabethan England – and Oxford was not particularly well educated.) Shakespeare received in the Stratford grammar school a formal education that would daunt many college graduates today; and popular rival playwrights such as the very learned Ben Jonson and George Chapman, both of whom also lacked university training, achieved great artistic success, without being taken as Bacon or Oxford.

Besides snobbery, one other quality characterizes the authorship controversy: lack of evidence. A great deal of testimony from Shakespeare's time shows that Shakespeare wrote Shakespeare's plays and that his contemporaries recognized them as distinctive and distinctly superior. (Some of that contemporary evidence is collected in E. K. Chambers, *William Shakespeare: A Study of Facts and Problems,* 2 vols., 1930.) Since that testimony comes from Shakespeare's enemies and theatrical competitors as well as from his co-workers and from the Elizabethan equivalent of literary journalists, it seems unlikely that, if any one of these sources had known he was a fraud, they would have failed to record that fact.

Books About Shakespeare's Theater

Useful scholarly studies of theatrical life in Shakespeare's day include: G. E. Bentley, *The Jacobean and Caroline Stage,* 7 vols. (1941-68), and the same author's *The Professions of Dramatist and Player in Shakespeare's Time, 1590-1642* (1986); E. K. Chambers, *The Elizabethan Stage,* 4 vols. (1923); R. A. Foakes, *Illustrations of the English Stage, 1580-1642* (1985); Andrew Gurr, *The Shakespearean Stage,* 3rd ed. (1992), and the same author's *Play-going in Shakespeare's London,* 2nd ed. (1996); Edwin Nungezer, *A Dictionary of Actors* (1929); Carol Chillington Rutter, ed., *Documents of the Rose Playhouse* (1984).

Books About Shakespeare's Life

The following books provide scholarly, documented accounts of Shakespeare's life: G. E. Bentley, *Shakespeare: A Biographical Handbook* (1961); E. K. Chambers, *William Shakespeare: A Study of Facts and Problems,* 2 vols. (1930); S. Schoenbaum, *William Shakespeare: A Compact*

Documentary Life (1977); and *Shakespeare's Lives,* 2nd ed. (1991), by the same author. Many scholarly editions of Shakespeare's complete works print brief compilations of essential dates and events. References to Shakespeare's works up to 1700 are collected in C. M. Ingleby et al., *The Shakespeare Allusion-Book,* rev. ed., 2 vols. (1932).

The Texts of Shakespeare

As far as we know, only one manuscript conceivably in Shakespeare's own hand may (and even this is much disputed) exist: a few pages of a play called *Sir Thomas More,* which apparently was never performed. What we do have, as later readers, performers, scholars, students, are printed texts. The earliest of these survive in two forms: quartos and folios. Quartos (from the Latin for "four") are small books, printed on sheets of paper that were then folded twice, to make four leaves or eight pages. When these were bound together, the result was a squarish, eminently portable volume that sold for the relatively small sum of sixpence (translating in modern terms to about $5.00). In folios, on the other hand, the sheets are folded only once, in half, producing large, impressive volumes taller than they are wide. This was the format for important works of philosophy, science, theology, and literature (the major precedent for a folio Shakespeare was Ben Jonson's *Works,* 1616). The decision to print the works of a popular playwright in folio is an indication of how far up on the social scale the theatrical profession had come during Shakespeare's lifetime. The Shakespeare folio was an expensive book, selling for between fifteen and eighteen shillings, depending on the binding (in modern terms, from about $150 to $180). Twenty Shakespeare plays of the thirty-seven that survive first appeared in quarto, seventeen of which appeared during Shakespeare's lifetime; the rest of the plays are found only in folio.

The First Folio was published in 1623, seven years after Shakespeare's death, and was authorized by his fellow actors, the co-owners of the King's Men. This publication

was certainly a mark of the company's enormous respect
for Shakespeare; but it was also a way of turning the old
plays, most of which were no longer current in the playhouse, into ready money (the folio includes only Shakespeare's plays, not his sonnets or other nondramatic verse).
Whatever the motives behind the publication of the folio,
the texts it preserves constitute the basis for almost all later
editions of the playwright's works. The texts, however, dif-
fer from those of the earlier quartos, sometimes in minor
respects but often significantly – most strikingly in the
two texts of *King Lear,* but also in important ways in
Hamlet, Othello, and *Troilus and Cressida.* (The variants
are recorded in the textual notes to each play in the new
Pelican series.) The differences in these texts represent, in
a sense, the essence of theater: the texts of plays were initially not intended for publication. They were scripts, designed for the actors to perform – the principal life of the
play at this period was in performance. And it follows that
in Shakespeare's theater the playwright typically had no
say either in how his play was performed or in the disposition of his text – he was an employee of the company. The
authoritative figures in the theatrical enterprise were the
shareholders in the company, who were for the most part
the major actors. They decided what plays were to be
done; they hired the playwright and often gave him an
outline of the play they wanted him to write. Often, too,
the play was a collaboration: the company would retain a
group of writers, and parcel out the scenes among them.
The resulting script was then the property of the company, and the actors would revise it as they saw fit during
the course of putting it on stage. The resulting text be-
longed to the company. The playwright had no rights in it
once he had been paid. (This system survives largely intact
in the movie industry, and most of the playwrights of
Shakespeare's time were as anonymous as most screenwrit-
ers are today.) The script could also, of course, continue to

change as the tastes of audiences and the requirements of
the actors changed. Many – perhaps most – plays were revised when they were reintroduced after any substantial
absence from the repertory, or when they were performed
by a company different from the one that originally com-
missioned the play.

Shakespeare was an exceptional figure in this world
because he was not only a shareholder and actor in his
company, but also its leading playwright – he was literally
his own boss. He had, moreover, little interest in the
publication of his plays, and even those that appeared
during his lifetime with the authorization of the company
show no signs of any editorial concern on the part of
the author. Theater was, for Shakespeare, a fluid and
supremely responsive medium – the very opposite of the
great classic canonical text that has embodied his works
since 1623.

The very fluidity of the original texts, however,
has meant that Shakespeare has always had to be edited.
Here is an example of how problematic the editorial pro-
ject inevitably is, a passage from the most famous speech
in *Romeo and Juliet,* Juliet's balcony soliloquy beginning
"O Romeo, Romeo, wherefore art thou Romeo?" Since
the eighteenth century, the standard modern text has
read,

> What's Montague? It is nor hand, nor foot,
> Nor arm, nor face, nor any other part
> Belonging to a man. O be some other name!
> What's in a name? That which we call a rose
> By any other name would smell as sweet.
> (II.2.40–44)

Editors have three early texts of this play to work from,
two quarto texts and the folio. Here is how the First
Quarto (1597) reads:

> Whats *Mountague*? It is nor band nor foote,
> Nor arme, nor face, nor any other part.
> Whats in a name? That which we call a Rofe,
> By any other name would fmell as fweet:

Here is the Second Quarto (1599):

> Whats *Mountague*? it is nor hand nor foote,
> Nor arme nor face, ô be fome other name
> Belonging to a man.
> Whats in a name that which we call a rofe,
> By any other word would fmell as fweete,

And here is the First Folio (1623):

> What's *Mountague*? it is nor hand nor foote,
> Nor arme, nor face, O be fome other name
> Belonging to a man.
> What? in a names that which we call a Rofe,
> By any other word would fmell as fweete,

There is in fact no early text that reads as our modern text does – and this is the most famous speech in the play. Instead, we have three quite different texts, all of which are clearly some version of the same speech, but none of which seems to us a final or satisfactory version. The transcendently beautiful passage in modern editions is an editorial invention: editors have succeeded in conflating and revising the three versions into something we recognize as great poetry. Is this what Shakespeare "really" wrote? Who can say? What we can say is that Shakespeare always had performance, not a book, in mind.

Books About the Shakespeare Texts

The standard study of the printing history of the First Folio is W. W. Greg, *The Shakespeare First Folio* (1955). J. K. Walton, *The Quarto Copy for the First Folio of Shakespeare* (1971), is a useful survey of the relation of the quartos to the folio. The second edition of Charlton Hinman's *Norton Facsimile* of the First Folio (1996), with a new introduction by Peter Blayney, is indispensable. Stanley Wells and Gary Taylor, *William Shakespeare: A Textual Companion,* keyed to the Oxford text, gives a comprehensive survey of the editorial situation for all the plays and poems.

THE GENERAL EDITORS

Introduction

SHAKESPEARE'S OVERWHELMING study of the tragedy of old age and the politics of the family has held the stage continuously since its first performance in 1606. In recent years it has rivaled *Hamlet* and *Romeo and Juliet* as the most frequently produced and intensely studied of Shakespeare's tragedies; its analysis of the disintegration of the closest family ties, the resentment and violence underlying the most intimate relationships, has seemed to speak to peculiarly modern concerns. In Shakespeare's own time it spoke as well to much larger political issues: the responsibilities of kingship, the continuity of rule, the unity of the commonwealth, and perhaps most troubling of all, the profound tenuousness of a patriarchal social order – of the assumption that the model for the commonwealth was the family, and that on all levels of society, father was king. Indeed, even overtly political tragedy, for Shakespeare, invariably starts in the family. It is Richard II's behavior toward his uncles and cousins that prompts the rebellion that deposes him; the tragedy of Hamlet begins with fratricide and incest, and takes shape around the complex relations of parents and children; Macbeth, assassinating Duncan at the urging of his wife, is murdering his first cousin; Lear's tragedy is from beginning to end a family matter. It is to the point that when James I came to the English throne in 1603, there was a fully constituted royal family at the center of English society for the first time since the death of Henry VIII. The first recorded performance of *King Lear,* on December 26, 1606, was at Whitehall Palace before King James – though the play seems to have been written in the previous year, the court performance may well have been the first, since plague had closed the public theaters for the season. If this is the case, Shakespeare's play began its life with Britain's royal patriarch at the center of its audience.

But the opening scene hardly mirrors the Jacobean court. Though the story of Lear comes from the chronicles of ancient Britain, the action belongs more to the world of legend than history. Lear's court initially seems like a fairy tale world, where momentous decisions are determined by trifles. The opening moments of the play invite us not to take the action seriously. The declarations of love Lear demands from his three daughters are to be performances, set pieces. Nothing apparently depends on them, since the division of the kingdom has already been decided upon – Lear arrives with a map already prepared. His daughters understand perfectly what is required of them; they have only to play their parts. Cordelia, refusing to produce her accolade, is disrupting both a courtly ceremonial and a family game, and it comes as a profound surprise to everyone present. In insisting on her right to silence, she is not only refusing to play, but is changing the rules.

How are we to take this scene? We could say that it is a debate between style and meaning, with Goneril and Regan showing their rhetorical art, and Cordelia, distrusting language, refusing to say what she does not believe. The older sisters' performances purport to be deeds, acts of homage to the king their father; but Cordelia objects that words are not deeds. From Goneril and Regan's perspective, these performances are noble ceremonies, hyperbolic and therefore appropriate responses to their royal father; from Cordelia's, they are merely specious shows, cheapening the king because they are inherently dishonest. If we look at the scene this way, it constitutes a debate between rhetoricians and plain-speakers, and it includes a good deal of the Elizabethan distrust of the theater as well – the fear that its representations will be taken for, and will thereby undermine or subvert, reality. Significantly here, it is the villains who are the performers.

We could look at the scene another way and say that the three sisters are being asked to sign a loyalty oath. Goneril and Regan agree to it because they are aware that the oath is really meaningless, and Cordelia refuses for exactly the same reason: because she too is aware that the oath is meaningless – the same perceptions can produce opposite actions, and motives for action are incalculable. The moral implications of the scene are immensely complicated because the issues are so trifling. Is Lear at fault for demanding the performance, for requiring the oath? As it turns out, he is, but we can imagine a different outcome, in which the willing adherence to the honorable forms of ceremonial behavior is seen as the essence of civilized society. These are precisely the values that Hamlet is nostalgic for, the old chivalric world, the world Macbeth destroys with his murder of Duncan. Whether Lear is at fault or not is almost beside the point: the point, as the scene proceeds, is much more schematic, and reminds us of Macbeth's world of paradoxes. The good daughter cannot express her love, while the bad daughters are believed; speech is lying and silence is truth; the richest reality is nothing – what Cordelia says, what her dowry is.

These issues relate to the larger question of the nature of power. In this scene about royalty and its dependencies, what constitutes power? In the case of the sisters, it is the ability to speak and please the king. The king's power is, to begin with, the power to bestow the monarchy. But Lear thinks of it in much less practical and more metaphysical ways, as the power of his senses –

Hence and avoid my sight! (125)

– and even more significantly, as the power of his language. Kent, urging Lear to rescind his decree, has sought "To come between our sentence and our power": a *sentence,* the crucial unit of structured language, is also the exercise of judicial authority. In our legal system, the full power of the law is still imposed by that word, "sentence." To punish criminals, we sentence them.

What Lear does *not* conceive his power to be is his position, the mere fact that he is king. But this, of course, is the sole source of his power, and he makes clear the way the drama is to move by resigning his office but nevertheless undertaking to retain "the name, and all th'addition to a king" (136). A question the play examines most intensely is what the name of king is – is it another nothing? What "addition" can a nothing have – what more than nothing is a nothing entitled to? And what is authority, which Kent sees in the face of the mad Lear? Can there be authority without power? What are the bases of judgment, essential for effective government? This question is central to *Macbeth,* too, as King Duncan observes of the thane who has betrayed him: "There's no art / To find the mind's construction in the face" (I.4 13-14).

Clearly the basis of judgment is not loyalty oaths. Even the victorious sisters realize how foolish Lear has been, observing, "with what poor judgment he hath cast [Cordelia] off appears too grossly" (290). More important is their observation that "he hath ever but slenderly known himself" (292-93); it implies that Lear's behavior is not simply a function of old age, but is both characteristic and at the heart of the play's disruptions. A king without self-knowledge is notoriously a danger to the commonwealth. But is Lear really responsible for the ensuing tragedy? How far could even the best of kings contain the villainy of Goneril, Regan, Cornwall, Edmund? Could Cordelia do so?

Moreover, though it is Kent who initially objects to Lear's bad judgment, only the villains assume that it renders him unfit to rule. In fact, elsewhere in the play Lear is referred to not as blind, foolish, irascible, self-centered, tyrannical, but as *kind* – Kent deplores "the hard rein which both of them have borne / Against the old kind king" (III.1.28). Lear on himself, "So kind a father!" (I.5.34), is presumably to be taken ironically, but his later characterization of himself, "Your old kind father, whose frank heart gave all" (III.4.20), is, objectively, true, though of course not the whole truth. When Richard Burbage, the leading tragedian of Shakespeare's company, died in 1618, his elegy listed the roles that made him famous:

> No more young Hamlet, old Hieronymo,
> Kind Lear, the grievèd Moor . . . *

The point here is not only that Lear is entitled to respect and pity, but even more significantly, that in a monarchy based on a philosophy of divine right, a bad king is still the king – Lear in fact never does give up his title: he is referred to as king throughout the play. This is no doubt why King James liked this tragedy about the extreme precariousness of kingship enough to have it performed at court. The play was, in this respect, for its original audiences, both politically conservative and basically sentimental. Modern audiences and critics who focus on Lear's irrationality and incompetence have adopted the point of view of the villains.

As Lear's plot derives from both ancient history and Jacobean politics, the parallel plot of Gloucester and his good and bad sons derives from contemporary romance. Shakespeare took the story from Sir Philip Sidney's immensely popular novel *Arcadia,* written in the 1580s, and an instant classic – by 1605 it had already gone through four editions. Gloucester's tragedy provides a running commentary on that of Lear and his daughters, but it also has its own momentum. Modern audiences find the casualness of Gloucester's attitude to Edmund's bastardy in

---

The Shakespeare Allusion Book, ed. John Munro (London: Oxford University Press, 1932), 1: 272.

the opening exchange with Kent at least disconcerting, if not reprehensible; but illegitimacy was a commonplace fact of Shakespeare's England, as it must be of any society without reliable methods of birth control, and though illegitimate children were barred from the line of succession and the inheritance of landed estates, no stigma was attached to the fact of bastardy itself. Noblemen freely acknowledged their illegitimate children, and often provided handsomely for them, and illegitimacy was no bar to social and political success: Elizabeth's powerful minister the Earl of Leicester was illegitimate, as were, technically, both Elizabeth herself and her predecessor on the throne Queen Mary I. Edmund complains of his bastardy, etymologizing it (incorrectly) from "base," but it is important to emphasize that he loses nothing on account of it. He is younger than the legitimate son Edgar, not older, and therefore even if he were not illegitimate, he would be entitled only to whatever his father chooses to give him: under the English law of primogeniture, the eldest son inherits the title, and the bulk of the estate. In fact, Edmund is contemptuous of his father precisely because he makes no distinction between his two sons, but loves and trusts them equally – contemptuous not because Gloucester is blind to the fact that Edmund is a bastard, but because he is blind to the fact that he is a villain.

But Edmund is more than a villain. He is in his way the great realist of the play. Invoking Nature as his goddess in a powerful soliloquy at the opening of Act I, scene 2, he defies conventional morality in favor of an ethic of pure self-interest. Shakespeare's contemporaries would have seen him as a Machiavellian figure, and to that extent a conventional stage villain; but what is probably most striking about him for us is the way he analyzes and overturns the idea of nature so central to the largest ethical claims of the play, the idea of nature as a benign and humane force. From Lear's and Cordelia's perspective, Goneril and Regan are behaving unnaturally; from Ed-

mund's, they are fulfilling nature's law, what we would call
the law of the jungle. It is Goneril and Regan who are the
play's conventional villains; Edmund is a genuinely subversive figure. He loses in the end, certainly, but so do
Lear and Cordelia; and what he introduces into the play is
a serious question about the basis of ethical behavior.

The Nature Edmund invokes is anarchic, full of com-
peting claims, not ordered and hierarchical. To acknowledge such a Nature is to acknowledge the reality, force,
and validity of the individual will – to acknowledge that
all of us have claims that conflict with claims about the
deference due to fathers and kings, about the hierarchy of
society and what is natural within the family. This is the
recognition that Edmund brings into *King Lear* when he
invokes Nature as his goddess. It is a Nature that is not
the image of divine order, but one in which the strongest
and craftiest survive – and when they survive, they then
go on to devise claims about Nature that justify their success, claims about hierarchies, natural law and order, the
divine right of kings, the sanctity of the father. Edmund is
a villain, but if he were ultimately successful he would
be indistinguishable from the Lears and Cordelias (and
James I's) of Shakespeare's world.

Such concerns may seem to us anachronistic: we tend
to believe that for Shakespeare's society the order of nature was a norm, the sanctity of patriarchy unquestion-
able. But ambivalence about what is natural within the
family was built into the very language of Elizabethan England: the alternative term for an illegitimate child was a
natural child – it is the legitimate, here, that is unnatural.
Edmund raises all the issues that Machiavelli had introduced into Renaissance political discourse, and the fear
generated by the figure of the Machiavel in Renaissance
England is a measure of how genuinely subversive those
issues were. The fact that Edmund must live by his wits,
that he is entitled only to what he can gain by his own efforts, actually makes him representative of a large segment

of Shakespeare's audience: his situation is not only that of bastards, but of every younger son in a culture that practices primogeniture. Edmund stands, disturbingly, at the center of the society's doubts about itself.

The ease with which Edmund's elder brother Edgar, Gloucester's legitimate heir, is displaced, is a measure of how forcefully those doubts were felt. Gloucester's whole sense of the beloved Edgar is overturned in an instant by Edmund's deception, as Lear's sense of Cordelia is overturned by a single act of obduracy. At the heart of the play, in both Lear's and Gloucester's families, is a conviction that human nature, even the nature of those closest to us, is essentially unknowable. Doubtless both Gloucester's and Edgar's gullibility are strongly contributing factors in the success of Edmund's schemes, but that gullibility stems precisely from their faith in the essential goodness and honesty of human nature. Would skepticism be sufficient protection against Edmund's villainy?

Once the enabling actions of the opening two scenes have occurred, the tragedy takes shape with extraordinary swiftness. Lear's reduction from monarch to "a poor old man, / As full of grief as age, wretched in both" (II.4.272-73) is complete by the end of Act II, the blinding of Gloucester by the end of Act III. The whole action of the play covers no more than a few weeks. It is not only the speed of this that is notable, but its violence, the abjectness of Lear's misery and madness, the savagery of Gloucester's treatment at the hands of Cornwall, Regan, and Goneril. The savagery is visited, moreover, not only on the characters, but on the audience as well: deaths, even murders, take place on Shakespeare's stage in every tragedy, but the blinding of Gloucester is all but unique – the closest parallel, the mutilation of Lavinia in *Titus Andronicus,* takes place offstage.

Along with the violence, the play has a strong erotic element, though it has little to do with the issues of marriage that fill the opening scene – "tell me how much you

love me" is what fathers say to children in this play, not
what lovers say to each other. The most powerful erotic
forces of the play are those of the villains, the adulterous
passion of Goneril and Regan for Edmund. It is this that
turns the sisters from natural allies to natural enemies.
Even so, the play includes no love scenes.

What, then, are the erotics of the opening scene? Burgundy and France have, after all, come to woo Cordelia,
but for both, the issue of inheritance is the primary one.
There is nothing culturally inappropriate about this: the
reason women in early modern cultures are provided with
dowries is that men will not marry them otherwise. In patriarchal societies, women are property, and no matter how
intelligent, accomplished, charming, or beautiful they may
be, the property is essential, and the more property they
represent the more desirable they are. Love is not irrelevant
to marriage, but neither is it the sole nor even the primary
consideration, and it is often represented as what follows
from a prosperous marriage, not what brings it about. Lear
dividing the kingdom among his three daughters, moreover, is following the dictates of English law: primogeniture applied exclusively to male heirs. If there were only
daughters, they inherited equally – Lear's willfulness in the
matter is manifested merely in his determination to give
Cordelia a better portion than her sisters.

Why then does Cordelia become more attractive to the
king of France when she is dowryless, and out of favor
with her father? This, in fact, is the romance element in
the plot: the love interest is represented as both chivalric
and quixotic. Of course, France's romantic passion can
also be seen cynically (or realistically), as representing basically an investment. The French king supporting, indeed, urging, an invasion of England by an army led by
his wife on behalf of his father-in-law is hardly disinterested. France is not concerned solely to get Lear in out of
the rain; to rescue Lear means repossessing at least
Cordelia's original third of the kingdom, and perhaps all

of it. Cordelia is a gamble, but in all the sources the gamble pays off handsomely: in Holinshed's *Chronicles,* from which Shakespeare took his history, Cordelia's army wins, Lear retrieves his throne, and Cordelia succeeds him. The surprise for a Jacobean audience would have been that in Shakespeare the gamble fails.

The parallel between Lear and Gloucester plays itself out as a double tragedy with two quite different morals. Both men are attended by the figures they have decisively rejected, either in disguise, like Kent and Edgar, or in the plain-speaking Fool, a surrogate Cordelia. Edgar leads his blind father out of despair through a little staged miracle, the extraordinary imagined fall from Dover Cliff in IV.6. But the resulting patience and acceptance lead to nothing but death, without even the recognition and reconciliation scene we have surely been primed to expect – and which is an essential element of the story in Shakespeare's source for the Gloucester plot, the episode of the Paphlagonian king in Sidney's *Arcadia* (Book 2, Chapter 10). In Sidney, the reconciliation has taken place even before the story is recounted, and is, in a sense, a determining condition of the story. Shakespeare's Edgar, almost at the play's end, merely reports that at the moment of Gloucester's death he did finally reveal his identity – the shock of recognition, in fact, is what killed Gloucester; but the announcement comes almost as an afterthought, the tying up of a loose end.

Gloucester is effectively abandoned by the play. His tragedy is framed, moreover, with a simplistic moral. Edgar, confronting Edmund at the end, says,

> The gods are just, and of our pleasant vices
> Make instruments to plague us.
> The dark and vicious place where thee he got
> Cost him his eyes.
>
> (V.3.172-75)

Edmund agrees: "Thou'st spoken right; 'tis true / The wheel is come full circle." But as a summation of Gloucester's tragedy, the lines seem singularly obtuse: Gloucester dies blaming his gullibility and imperceptiveness; he never gives any sign of regret for his youthful adultery. We will be especially unpersuaded by Edgar's conviction of the economy of divine justice if we think of Cordelia's fate, and even of Lear's, which seem more appropriately summed up with Gloucester's own cosmic epigram,

> As flies to wanton boys are we to th' gods;
> They kill us for their sport.
>
> (IV.1.36-37)

Tragedy may be a moralizing form, but it is not an equitable one: the innocent invariably suffer with the guilty, and often more than the guilty. If tragedy has a moral, it is surely that we *do not* get what we deserve. We might contrast the sense Edgar makes of his tragedy with the sense Cordelia, stoical in defeat, makes of hers: "We are not the first / Who with best meaning have incurred the worst" (V.3.3-4).

In the tragedy of Lear and Cordelia, the moral is obscure but the suffering and awareness are the measures of value. Renaissance philosophy and theology almost without exception took the position of Lear and Cordelia. Edgar's notion of cosmic justice would have been considered to be like a belief in horoscopes, naive and simplistic. Providence works on far too vast a scale for individual suffering to be included in it – the heavens do not provide comfort: that one must make for oneself. Virtue, proverbial wisdom tells us, is its own reward: the virtuous gain nothing but the thing itself, the knowledge that they are virtuous. This is not a philosophy designed to produce happy endings.

Renaissance Christianity was not a cozy or friendly faith; whether Protestant or Catholic, the church was fierce and uncompromising, not the welcoming mother one could always return to, but an omnipotent and largely disapproving father. The notion of a comforting Christianity, gentle Jesus meek and mild, is a relatively modern development; for Milton, God's ways have to be *justified* to man, and the task is not an easy one.

In the final scene we find Lear creating a play world, the reconciliation with Cordelia allowing nothing more than a childish fantasy:

> Come, let's away to prison.
> We two alone will sing like birds i' th' cage.
> (V.3.8-9)

The point about birds in a cage is that they are happier than we are. Lear conceives of themselves getting clear out of the world of action and passion, spies for a God who has left the world unattended (why else would God needs spies?), and thus creating the only permanence in a world of change. Of course this is a fantasy, not merely because of the real pathos of Lear's condition, but because it leaves out of account all the other realities of his world – the villainy of Edmund, who has ordered them killed, but also the realities of what even the men of good will in this play are like. Albany has to be *reminded* by Kent of the king and Cordelia, and he replies, "Great thing of us forgot" (236). Forgetting a great thing makes it a nothing. Cordelia and Lear are killed as much by passive forgetfulness as by active villainy. Even in the play's last moments, lack of awareness is the destructive element.

Albany's pious prayer, "The gods defend her" (257), is immediately followed by Lear carrying Cordelia's corpse, howling like a beast; and it seems to Kent and Edgar the Day of Judgment – "Is this the promised end?" "Or image of that horror?" (263-64) – though characteristically it seems real to Kent, an image to Edgar. For Lear now, the only possible redemption is that Cordelia might not be dead. For a moment he thinks that she is alive, cruelly deceived; and then, when it is clear that she is not, raging again, he accuses the best and most faithful of friends, Kent and Edgar, of having murdered her. Good will counts for nothing, nothing redeems sorrows; Kent says it: "All's cheerless, dark, and deadly" (296). The final realization, the final truth of plain-speaking, is five *nevers:*

> Thou'lt come no more,
> Never, never, never, never, never.
> (314-15)

Lear heartbreakingly extends Cordelia's *nothing* into the scheme of time. He returns momentarily to the fantasy that she lives – "Look on her! Look, her lips!" – and with that false hope he dies.

It is important to emphasize that the exceptional bleakness of this conclusion is all Shakespeare's. In the story as he found it in every one of the sources, Cordelia's army is victorious, and Lear reascends his throne. Kent's simple eulogy does no more than accept the facts, and proposes no moral:

> He hates him
> That would upon the rack of this tough world
> Stretch him out longer.

The world is an instrument of torture, and the only comfort is in the nothing, the never, of death. The heroic vision is of suffering, unredeemed and unmitigated. Kent says, "The wonder is, he hath endured so long."

STEPHEN ORGEL
Stanford University

Note on the Text

KING LEAR HAS COME down to us in two significantly different versions, a quarto published in 1608 and the text printed in the first folio of 1623. Each of these includes material missing from the other: the folio has 115 lines not in the quarto, while the quarto has 285 lines (including a whole scene, and a large part of another) not in the folio. There are many smaller variations as well, in individual words, speech designations, lineation. It is generally, though not universally, agreed now that the quarto represents a version of the heavily corrected and revised manuscript that came from Shakespeare's hand, and that the folio represents a later performing version of the play. The implication is that the quarto represents the play *before* it was performed, the play as it went to the acting company to be transcribed and turned into a performing text, and that the folio version represents the performing text, though not necessarily the only version the company had performed in the years between 1605 and 1623.

Since Lewis Theobald's edition of Shakespeare's plays, published in 1733, the standard text of *King Lear* has been a conflation of the quarto and folio texts, with the presumption being that both are cut versions of a longer original. Because the two texts disagree on many matters, however, it is not possible simply to combine them, and a good deal of editorial judgment has always been required to produce a final version. Even editors who do not believe that behind the two texts lies a single Shakespearean original have nevertheless preferred a conflated text simply because it gives us more Shakespeare – the quarto, indeed, is our only source for one of the most famous moments in the play, Lear's mock-trial of his daughters in

III.6, and even if we believe Shakespeare edited this out of the final script, it is a scene later actors, directors, and editors have been loath to lose.

The play as presented in this volume is the traditional conflated text. It is substantially that prepared by Alfred Harbage for the old Pelican series, which in turn derives ultimately from the eighteenth-century text established by Theobald. (New glosses and notes have been provided.) Passages found only in the quarto are enclosed in roman brackets. For readers who wish to read the play in its two separate states, a companion volume in this series includes a two-text *King Lear,* with a discussion of the differences, and full textual notes.

King Lear

[Names of the Actors

LEAR, *King of Britain*
KING OF FRANCE
GONERIL, *Lear's eldest daughter*
DUKE OF ALBANY, *Goneril's husband*
REGAN, *Lear's second daughter*
DUKE OF CORNWALL, *Regan's husband*
CORDELIA, *Lear's youngest daughter*
DUKE OF BURGUNDY
EARL OF KENT
EARL OF GLOUCESTER
EDGAR, *Gloucester's elder son, later disguised as*
    Tom o' Bedlam
EDMUND, *Gloucester's younger, bastard son*
OSWALD, *Goneril's steward*
OLD MAN, *Gloucester's tenant*
CURAN, *Gloucester's servant*
FOOL, *attending on Lear*
DOCTOR
SERVANTS, CAPTAINS, HERALD, KNIGHTS,
    MESSENGERS, GENTLEMEN, SOLDIERS, *etc.*

SCENE: *Britain*]
*

King Lear

I.1 *Enter Kent, Gloucester, and Edmund.*

KENT I thought the king had more affected the Duke of   1
Albany than Cornwall.   2

GLOUCESTER It did always seem so to us; but now, in the
division of the kingdom, it appears not which of the
dukes he values most, for equalities are so weighed that   5
curiosity in neither can make choice of either's moiety.   6

KENT Is not this your son, my lord?

GLOUCESTER His breeding, sir, hath been at my charge.
I have so often blushed to acknowledge him that now I
am brazed to't.   10

KENT I cannot conceive you.   11

GLOUCESTER Sir, this young fellow's mother could;
whereupon she grew round-wombed, and had indeed,
sir, a son for her cradle ere she had a husband for her
bed. Do you smell a fault?

KENT I cannot wish the fault undone, the issue of it
being so proper.   17

GLOUCESTER But I have a son, sir, by order of law, some   18
year elder than this who yet is no dearer in my account: 19
though this knave came something saucily to the world   20
before he was sent for, yet was his mother fair, there was

I.1 Lear's palace **s.d.** *Gloucester* (pronounced "Gloster") **1–2** *more affected . . . than* preferred . . . to **2** *Albany* i.e., Scotland **5** *equalities . . .
weighed* their qualities are so equal **6** *curiosity . . . moiety* thorough exami-
nation cannot find either's share preferable **10** *brazed* brazened **11** *conceive* understand **17** *proper* handsome **18** *by . . . law* legitimate **19**
account esteem **20** *something saucily* somewhat impertinently

22   good sport at his making, and the whoreson must be
     acknowledged. Do you know this noble gentleman,
     Edmund?

EDMUND   No, my lord.

GLOUCESTER   My lord of Kent. Remember him hereafter
     as my honorable friend.

EDMUND   My services to your lordship.

29   KENT   I must love you, and sue to know you better.

30   EDMUND   Sir, I shall study deserving. *foregrounds his shift*

31   GLOUCESTER   He hath been out nine years, and away he
32   shall again.
             [Sound a] sennet.
         The king is coming.
             Enter [one bearing a coronet, then] King Lear, [then
             the Dukes of] Cornwall, [and] Albany, [next] Goneril,
             Regan, Cordelia, and Attendants.

LEAR
     Attend the lords of France and Burgundy, Gloucester.

GLOUCESTER
     I shall, my lord.   *Exit [with Edmund].*

LEAR   *→ pun: he has no idea*
36   Meantime we shall express our darker purpose. *how dark it*
     Give me the map there. Know that we have divided *will be*
38   In three our kingdom; and 'tis our fast intent
     To shake all cares and business from our age,
40   Conferring them on younger strengths while we
41   Unburdened crawl toward death. Our son of Cornwall,
     And you our no less loving son of Albany,
43   We have this hour a constant will to publish
44   Our daughters' several dowers, that future strife
     May be prevented now. The princes, France and Bur-
         gundy,

---

22 *whoreson* literally "bastard," but the word was also an affectionate term,
like "scamp" **29** *sue* seek **30** *study deserving* undertake to deserve it **31**
out away **32 s.d.** *sennet* trumpet fanfare **36** *darker purpose* secret plan **38**
fast intent firm intention **41** *son* son-in-law **43** *constant . . . publish* determination to express publicly **44** *several dowers* individual dowries

Great rivals in our youngest daughter's love,
Long in our court have made their amorous sojourn,
And here are to be answered. Tell me, my daughters
(Since now we will divest us both of rule,
Interest of territory, cares of state),   *comes from a place[50] of insecurity?*
Which of you shall we say doth love us most,
That we our largest bounty may extend
Where nature doth with merit challenge. Goneril,   53
Our eldest born, speak first.   *love is merit*

GONERIL
Sir, I love you more than word can wield the matter;   55
Dearer than eyesight, space, and liberty; → *ironic*   56
Beyond what can be valued, rich or rare; *she doesn't have*
No less than life, with grace, health, beauty, honor; *any of*
As much as child e'er loved, or father found; *these but*
A love that makes breath poor, and speech unable. *might*
Beyond all manner of so much I love you.   *soon*

CORDELIA   *[Aside]*
What shall Cordelia speak? Love, and be silent.

LEAR
Of all these bounds, even from this line to this,
With shadowy forests and with champains riched,   64
With plenteous rivers and wide-skirted meads,   65
We make thee lady. To thine and Albany's issues   66
Be this perpetual. – What says our second daughter,
Our dearest Regan, wife of Cornwall?

REGAN
I am made of that self mettle as my sister,   69
And prize me at her worth. In my true heart   70
I find she names my very deed of love;
Only she comes too short, that I profess   72
Myself an enemy to all other joys

---

50 *Interest of* legal title to   **53** *nature . . . challenge* the claims of natural affection are as strong as those of merit   **55** *wield the matter* express the subject
56 *space* scope (to enjoy "liberty")   **60** *breath* voice   **64** *shadowy* shady;
champains riched cultivated plains   **65** *wide-skirted meads* spreading mead-
ows   **66** *issues* heirs   **69** *self* same   **70** *prize me* value myself   **72** *that* in that

74 Which the most precious square of sense possesses,
75 And find I am alone felicitate
In your dear highness' love.

CORDELIA *[Aside]*   Then poor Cordelia;
And yet not so, since I am sure my love's
More ponderous than my tongue.

LEAR
To thee and thine hereditary ever
80 Remain this ample third of our fair kingdom,
81 No less in space validity, and pleasure
Than that conferred on Goneril. – Now, our joy,
83 Although our last and least, to whose young love
The vines of France and milk of Burgundy
85 Strive to be interested, what can you say to draw
A third more opulent than your sisters? Speak.

CORDELIA Nothing, my lord.

LEAR Nothing?

CORDELIA Nothing.

LEAR   → book is proof of the opposite
90 Nothing will come of nothing. Speak again.

CORDELIA
Unhappy that I am, I cannot heave
My heart into my mouth. I love your majesty
93 According to my bond, no more nor less.

LEAR
How, how, Cordelia? Mend your speech a little,
Lest you may mar your fortunes.

CORDELIA   Good my lord,
96 You have begot me, bred me, loved me. I
Return those duties back as are right fit,
Obey you, love you, and most honor you.
Why have my sisters husbands if they say

---

74 *most . . . possesses* measure of perception holds to be most precious (?) 75 *felicitate* made happy 81 *validity* value 83 *least* smallest 85 *interested* entitled to a share 90 *Nothing . . . nothing* (quoting a famous scholastic maxim derived from Aristotle, *nihil ex nihilo fit*) 93 *bond* duty 96–97 *I . . . fit* I am properly dutiful in return

They love you all? Haply, when I shall wed,   *100*
That lord whose hand must take my plight shall carry   101
Half my love with him, half my care and duty.
Sure I shall never marry like my sisters,
[To love my father all.]
LEAR   But goes thy heart with this?
CORDELIA   Ay, my good lord.
LEAR   So young, and so untender?
CORDELIA   So young, my lord, and true.   108
LEAR
Let it be so, thy truth then be thy dower!
For, by the sacred radiance of the sun,   110
The mysteries of Hecate and the night,   111
By all the operation of the orbs   112
From whom we do exist and cease to be,
Here I disclaim all my paternal care,
Propinquity, and property of blood,   115
And as a stranger to my heart and me
Hold thee from this forever. The barbarous Scythian,   117
Or he that makes his generation messes   118
To gorge his appetite, shall to my bosom
Be as well neighbored, pitied, and relieved,   *120*
As thou my sometime daughter.
KENT   Good my liege –
LEAR
Peace, Kent!
Come not between the dragon and his wrath.
I loved her most, and thought to set my rest
On her kind nursery. – Hence and avoid my sight! –   125
So be my grave my peace as here I give   126
Her father's heart from her! Call France. Who stirs!

---

101 *plight* marriage vow 108 *true* honest 111 *Hecate* goddess of the un-
derworld and patron of witchcraft 112 *operation . . . orbs* astrological influ-
ences 115 *Propinquity . . . blood* blood relationship 117 *this* this time;
Scythian Crimean tribesman, notorious for cruelty 118 *makes . . . messes*
devours his children 125 *nursery* care 126 *So . . . peace* let my only peace
be in my grave

Call Burgundy. Cornwall and Albany,
With my two daughters' dowers digest the third;
130 Let pride, which she calls plainness, marry her.
I do invest you jointly with my power,
132 Preeminence, and all the large effects
133 That troop with majesty. Ourself, by monthly course,
134 With reservation of an hundred knights,
By you to be sustained, shall our abode
Make with you by due turn. Only we shall retain
137 The name, and all th' addition to a king. The sway,
Revenue, execution of the rest,
Belovèd sons, be yours; which to confirm,
140 This coronet part between you.

KENT   Royal Lear,
Whom I have ever honored as my king,
Loved as my father, as my master followed,
As my great patron thought on in my prayers –

LEAR
144 The bow is bent and drawn; make from the shaft.

KENT
145 Let it fall rather, though the fork invade
The region of my heart. Be Kent unmannerly
When Lear is mad. What wouldst thou do, old man?
Think'st thou that duty shall have dread to speak
149 When power to flattery bows? To plainness honor's
bound
150 When majesty falls to folly. Reserve thy state,
And in thy best consideration check
152 This hideous rashness. Answer my life my judgment,
Thy youngest daughter does not love thee least,

---

132 *large effects* rich trappings   133 *troop with* accompany; *by . . . course*
month by month   134 *With reservation of* legally retaining   137 *all th' addition* i.e., the honors and prerogatives; *sway* authority   140 *coronet* (which
would have crowned Cordelia)   144 *make from* get out of the way of   145
fall strike; *fork* (two-pronged) arrowhead   149 *plainness* straight talk   150
Reserve . . . state retain your authority   152 *Answer my life* I stake my life on

Nor are those empty-hearted whose low sounds
Reverb no hollowness.   155
LEAR   Kent, on thy life, no more!
KENT
My life I never held but as a pawn   157
To wage against thine enemies; ne'er fear to lose it,   158
Thy safety being motive.   159
LEAR   Out of my sight!   160
KENT
See better, Lear, and let me still remain   161
The true blank of thine eye.   162
LEAR   Now by Apollo –   163
KENT
Now by Apollo, king,
Thou swear'st thy gods in vain.
LEAR   O vassal! Miscreant!   *[Grasping his sword]*   166
ALBANY, CORNWALL   Dear sir, forbear!   167
KENT
Kill thy physician, and thy fee bestow
Upon the foul disease. Revoke thy gift,
Or, whilst I can vent clamor from my throat,   170
I'll tell thee thou dost evil.   171
LEAR   Hear me, recreant,
On thine allegiance, hear me!
That thou hast sought to make us break our vows,   173
Which we durst never yet, and with strained pride   174
To come betwixt our sentence and our power,   175
Which nor our nature nor our place can bear,   176
Our potency made good, take thy reward.   177

---

155 *Reverb no hollowness* do not resonate hollowly   157 *pawn* both stake
and the least valuable chess piece   158 *wage* wager, risk   159 *motive* moti-
vation   161 *still* always   162 *true blank* exact bull's-eye   163 *Apollo* the sun
god   166 *Miscreant* both villain and infidel   167 *Cornwall* (or Cordelia: F's
speech heading is *Cor.*)   171 *recreant* traitor   173 *That* since   174 *strained*
excessive   175 *our power* the power to execute it   176 *place* royal office
177 *Our . . . good* hereby demonstrating my power

Five days we do allot thee for provision
To shield thee from disasters of the world,
180 And on the sixth to turn thy hated back
Upon our kingdom. If, on the tenth day following,
182 Thy banished trunk be found in our dominions,
The moment is thy death. Away! By Jupiter,
This shall not be revoked.

KENT
185 Fare thee well, king. Sith thus thou wilt appear,
Freedom lives hence, and banishment is here.
      [To Cordelia]
The gods to their dear shelter take thee, maid,
That justly think'st and hast most rightly said.
      [To Regan and Goneril]
189 And your large speeches may your deeds approve,
190 That good effects may spring from words of love.
Thus Kent, O princes, bids you all adieu;
192 He'll shape his old course in a country new.   *Exit.*
      Flourish. Enter Gloucester, with France and Burgundy,
      Attendants.

GLOUCESTER
Here's France and Burgundy, my noble lord.

LEAR
My lord of Burgundy,
We first address toward you, who with this king
Hath rivaled for our daughter. What in the least
Will you require in present dower with her,
Or cease your quest of love?

BURGUNDY   Most royal majesty,
I crave no more than hath your highness offered,
200 Nor will you tender less.

LEAR   Right noble Burgundy,
When she was dear to us, we did hold her so;

_____
182 *trunk* body   **185** *Sith* since   **189** *your . . . approve* i.e., may your actions
justify your words   **192 s.d.** *Flourish* fanfare   **200** *tender* offer

But now her price is fallen. Sir, there she stands.
If aught within that little seeming substance,   203
Or all of it, with our displeasure pieced   204
And nothing more, may fitly like your grace,   205
She's there, and she is yours.
BURGUNDY   I know no answer.
LEAR
Will you, with those infirmities she owes,   207
Unfriended, new-adopted to our hate,
Dowered with our curse, and strangered with our oath,   209
Take her or leave her?   210
BURGUNDY   Pardon me, royal sir;
Election makes not up on such conditions.   211
LEAR   *wealth vs. value*
Then leave her, sir, for by the power that made me
I tell you all her wealth. *[To France]* For you, great king,
I would not from your love make such a stray   214
To match you where I hate; therefore beseech you
T' avert your liking a more worthier way   *asks the king*
Than on a wretch whom Nature is ashamed   *of France not*
Almost t' acknowledge hers.   *to marry her*
FRANCE   This is most strange,
That she whom even but now was your best object,
The argument of your praise, balm of your age,   220
The best, the dearest, should in this trice of time
Commit a thing so monstrous to dismantle   222
So many folds of favor. Sure her offense
Must be of such unnatural degree
That monsters it, or your forevouched affection   225

---

203 *aught* anything; *little . . . substance* both mere shell of a person and person with few pretensions   **204** *pieced* joined   **205** *like* please   **207** *owes* owns   **209** *strangered with* made a stranger by   **211** *Election . . . conditions* choice is impossible on such terms   **214** *make . . . stray* stray so far as   **216** *avert* turn   **220** *argument* theme   **222** *to dismantle* as to strip off   **225** *monsters it* makes it monstrous   **225–226** *your . . . taint* the love you previously swore must now appear suspect

Fall into taint; which to believe of her
Must be a faith that reason without miracle
Should never plant in me.

CORDELIA   *[To Lear]*   I yet beseech your majesty,
229   If for I want that glib and oily art
230   To speak and purpose not, since what I well intend
I'll do't before I speak, that you make known
It is no vicious blot, murder, or foulness,
No unchaste action or dishonored step
That hath deprived me of your grace and favor;
But even for want of that for which I am richer—
236   A still-soliciting eye, and such a tongue
That I am glad I have not, though not to have it
Hath lost me in your liking.

LEAR   Better thou
Hadst not been born than not t' have pleased me better.

FRANCE
240   Is it but this? A tardiness in nature
Which often leaves the history unspoke
That it intends to do. My lord of Burgundy,
What say you to the lady? Love's not love
244   When it is mingled with regards that stands
Aloof from th' entire point. Will you have her?
She is herself a dowry.

BURGUNDY   Royal king,
Give but that portion which yourself proposed,
And here I take Cordelia by the hand,
Duchess of Burgundy.

LEAR
250   Nothing. I have sworn. I am firm.

BURGUNDY
I am sorry then you have so lost a father
That you must lose a husband.

---

229 *for I want* because I lack   **236** *still-soliciting* always begging   **244–45**
regards . . . point considerations irrelevant to love

CORDELIA
Peace be with Burgundy.
Since that respects of fortune are his love,   254
I shall not be his wife.

FRANCE
Fairest Cordelia, that art most rich being poor,
Most choice forsaken, and most loved despised,
Thee and thy virtues here I seize upon.
Be it lawful I take up what's cast away.
Gods, gods! 'Tis strange that from their cold'st neglect   *260*
My love should kindle to inflamed respect.   261
Thy dowerless daughter, king, thrown to my chance,
Is queen of us, of ours, and our fair France.
Not all the dukes of wat'rish Burgundy   264
Can buy this unprized precious maid of me.   265
Bid them farewell, Cordelia, though unkind.
Thou losest here, a better where to find.   267

LEAR
Thou hast her, France; let her be thine, for we
Have no such daughter, nor shall ever see
That face of hers again. Therefore be gone,   *270*
Without our grace, our love, our benison.   271
Come, noble Burgundy.
     Flourish. Exeunt [Lear, Burgundy, Cornwall, Albany,
     Gloucester, and Attendants].

FRANCE
Bid farewell to your sisters.

CORDELIA
The jewels of our father, with washed eyes   274
Cordelia leaves you. I know you what you are;
And, like a sister, am most loath to call
Your faults as they are named. Love well our father.   277

---

254 *respects . . . fortune* considerations of wealth   **261** *inflamed respect* ardent
admiration   **264** *wat'rish* (1) well irrigated, (2) weak, wishy-washy   **265** *unprized* unappreciated   **267** *where* elsewhere   **271** *benison* blessing   **274**
washed tearful   **277** *as . . . named* by their real names

278 To your professèd bosoms I commit him;
But yet, alas, stood I within his grace,
280 I would prefer him to a better place.
So farewell to you both.

REGAN
Prescribe not us our duty.

GONERIL   Let your study
Be to content your lord, who hath received you
284 At fortune's alms. You have obedience scanted,
285 And well are worth the want that you have wanted.

CORDELIA *"time will bring things to light"*
Time shall unfold what plighted cunning hides,
287 Who covers faults, at last with shame derides.
Well may you prosper.

FRANCE   Come, my fair Cordelia.

Exit France and Cordelia.

GONERIL   Sister, it is not little I have to say of what most
290 nearly appertains to us both. I think our father will
hence tonight.

REGAN   That's most certain, and with you; next month
with us.

GONERIL   You see how full of changes his age is. The observation we have made of it hath not been little. He always loved our sister most and with what poor
297 judgment he hath now cast her off appears too grossly.

REGAN   'Tis the infirmity of his age; yet he hath ever but
slenderly known himself.

300 GONERIL   The best and soundest of his time hath been
301 but rash; then must we look from his age to receive not
302 alone the imperfections of long-ingraffed condition,

[marginal note, left: "advised of changes"]

---

278 *professèd bosoms* proclaimed love   280 *prefer* promote   284 *At . . . alms*
as charity from fortune   285 *well . . . wanted* are properly deprived of what
you yourself have lacked   287 *Who . . . derides* i.e., time finally exposes hidden faults to shame   297 *grossly* obviously   300 *The . . . been* even at his
best he was   301 *then* therefore   302 *long-ingraffed* deep-seated

but therewithal the unruly waywardness that infirm   303
and choleric years bring with them.

REGAN   Such unconstant starts are we like to have from   305
him as this of Kent's banishment.

GONERIL   There is further compliment of leave-taking   307
between France and him. Pray you let us hit together; if   308
our father carry authority with such disposition as he
bears, this last surrender of his will but offend us.   310

REGAN   We shall further think of it.

GONERIL   We must do something, and i' th' heat.   312

           Exeunt.

*

∾ **I.2** *Enter Bastard [Edmund, solus, with a letter].*

EDMUND   *law is not subject to nature*
Thou, Nature, art my goddess; to thy law
My services are bound. Wherefore should I
<u>Stand</u> in the plague of custom, and permit   3
The curiosity of nations to deprive me,   4
For that I am some twelve or fourteen moonshines   5
Lag of a brother? Why bastard? Wherefore base,   6
When my dimensions are as well compact,   7
My mind as generous, and my shape as true,   8
As honest madam's issue? Why brand they us   9
With base? with baseness? Bastardy base? Base?   10
Who, in the lusty stealth of nature, take   11
More composition and fierce quality   12

---

303 *therewithal* along with that   **305** *unconstant starts* fits of impulsiveness
307 *compliment* formality   **308** *hit* consult   **310** *last surrender* recent abdi-
cation   **312** *i' th' heat* immediately ("while the iron is hot")
 I.2 Gloucester's house   **3** *Stand . . . custom* submit to the affliction of
convention (whereby the eldest son inherits everything, and illegitimate sons
have no claim on the estate)   **4** *curiosity* (legal) technicalities   **5** *For that* because; *moonshines* months   **6** *Lag of* younger than   **7** *compact* composed   **8**
My . . . generous I am as well supplied with intelligence   **9** *honest* chaste (i.e.,
married)   **11** *the . . . nature* natural lust practiced in secret   **12** *composition*
physical excellence; *fierce* vigorous

Than doth, within a dull, stale, tired bed,
14 Go to th' creating a whole tribe of fops
15 Got 'tween asleep and wake? Well then,
16 Legitimate Edgar, I must have your land.
Our father's love is to the bastard Edmund
As to th' legitimate. Fine word, "legitimate."
19 Well, my legitimate, if this letter speed,
20 And my invention thrive, Edmund the base
Shall top th' legitimate. I grow, I prosper.
Now, gods, stand up for bastards.
Enter Gloucester. [Edmund reads a letter.]
GLOUCESTER
23 Kent banished thus? and France in choler parted?
24 And the king gone tonight? prescribed his pow'r?
25 Confined to exhibition? All this done
26 Upon the gad? – Edmund, how now? What news?
EDMUND   So please your lordship, none.
GLOUCESTER   Why so earnestly seek you to put up that
letter?
30 EDMUND   I know no news, my lord.
GLOUCESTER   What paper were you reading?
EDMUND   Nothing, my lord.
33 GLOUCESTER   No? What needed then that terrible dispatch of it into your pocket? The quality of nothing
hath not such need to hide itself. Let's see. Come, if it
be nothing, I shall not need spectacles.
EDMUND   I beseech you, sir, pardon me. It is a letter
from my brother that I have not all o'erread; and for so
much as I have perused, I find it not fit for your o'er-
40 looking.
GLOUCESTER   Give me the letter, sir.

---

14 *fops* fools, sissies   15 *Got* begotten   16 *land* i.e., inheritance   19 *speed*
succeed   20 *invention* scheme   23 *in . . . parted* departed in anger   24
tonight i.e., last night; *prescribed . . . pow'r* told how much power he is to have
25 *Confined . . . exhibition* limited to an allowance   26 *Upon . . . gad* suddenly, impulsively   33 *terrible* frightened

EDMUND   I shall offend, either to detain or give it. The
contents, as in part I understand them, are to blame.   43
GLOUCESTER   Let's see, let's see.
EDMUND   I hope, for my brother's justification, he wrote
this but as an essay or taste of my virtue.   46
GLOUCESTER   *Reads.* "This policy and reverence of age   47
makes the world bitter to the best of our times; keeps   48
our fortunes from us till our oldness cannot relish
them. I begin to find an idle and fond bondage in the   50
oppression of aged tyranny, who sways, not as it hath
power, but as it is suffered. Come to me, that of this I   52
may speak more. If our father would sleep till I waked
him, you should enjoy half his revenue forever, and live
the beloved of your brother.   Edgar."
Hum! Conspiracy? "Sleep till I waked him, you should
enjoy half his revenue." My son Edgar! Had he a hand
to write this? A heart and brain to breed it in? When
came you to this? Who brought it?
EDMUND   It was not brought me, my lord; there's the   60
cunning of it. I found it thrown in at the casement of   61
my closet.
GLOUCESTER   You know the character to be your   63
brother's?
EDMUND   If the matter were good, my lord, I durst swear   65
it were his; but in respect of that, I would fain think it   66
were not.
GLOUCESTER   It is his.
EDMUND   It is his hand, my lord; but I hope his heart is
not in the contents.   70

---

43 *to blame* blameworthy   46 *essay . . . taste* (both words mean test)   47
policy . . . of policy of reverence for   48 *to . . . times* in the prime of our lives
50 *idle . . . fond* worthless and foolish   52 *suffered* allowed to do so   61–62
casement . . . closet window of my bedroom   63 *character* handwriting   65
matter substance   66 *in . . . that* i.e., considering the content; *fain* prefer to

71 GLOUCESTER Has he never before sounded you in this
business?

EDMUND Never, my lord. But I have heard him oft
74 maintain it to be fit that, sons at perfect age, and fa-
75 thers declined, the father should be as ward to the son,
and the son manage his revenue. *vs. daughters*

GLOUCESTER O villain, villain! His very opinion in the
letter. Abhorred villain, unnatural, detested, brutish vil-
79 lain; worse than brutish! Go, sirrah, seek him. I'll ap-
80 prehend him. Abominable villain! Where is he?

EDMUND I do not well know, my lord. If it shall please
you to suspend your indignation against my brother
till you can derive from him better testimony of his in-
84 tent, you should run a certain course; where, if you vi-
olently proceed against him, mistaking his purpose, it
would make a great gap in your own honor and shake
87 in pieces the heart of his obedience. I dare pawn down
88 my life for him that he hath writ this to feel my affec-
89 tion to your honor, and to no other pretense of danger.

90 GLOUCESTER Think you so?

91 EDMUND If your honor judge it meet, I will place you
92 where you shall hear us confer of this and by an auricu-
lar assurance have your satisfaction, and that without
any further delay than this very evening.

GLOUCESTER He cannot be such a monster.

[EDMUND Nor is not, sure.

GLOUCESTER To his father, that so tenderly and entirely
loves him. Heaven and earth!] Edmund, seek him out;
99 wind me into him, I pray you; frame the business after

---

71 *sounded you* sounded you out   74 *sons . . . age* when sons are mature   75
as . . . to placed under the guardianship of   79 *sirrah* (term of address used
to a child or social inferior)   84 *run . . . course* be sure of your course of action; *where* whereas   87 *pawn down* stake   88 *feel* test   89 *pretense of danger* intent to do harm   91 *meet* appropriate   92–93 *an . . . assurance* the
testimony of your own ears   99 *wind . . . him* worm your way into his con-
fidence for me; *frame* arrange

your own wisdom. I would unstate myself to be in a   100
due resolution.

EDMUND   I will seek him, sir, presently; convey the busi-   102
ness as I shall find means, and acquaint you withal.   103

GLOUCESTER   These late eclipses in the sun and moon   104
portend no good to us. Though the wisdom of nature   105
can reason it thus and thus, yet nature finds itself   106
scourged by the sequent effects. Love cools, friendship
falls off, brothers divide. In cities, mutinies; in coun-   108
tries, discord; in palaces, treason; and the bond cracked
'twixt son and father. This villain of mine comes under   110
the prediction, there's son against father; the king falls   111
from bias of nature, there's father against child. We   112
have seen the best of our time. Machinations,
hollowness, treachery, and all ruinous disorders follow   114
us disquietly to our graves. Find out this villain, Edmund; it shall lose thee nothing; do it carefully. And
the noble and true-hearted Kent banished; his offense,
honesty. 'Tis strange. →also notices Lear's   Exit.   madness

[margin: natural 2,]

EDMUND   This is the excellent foppery of the world, that   119
when we are sick in fortune, often the surfeits of our own   120
behavior, we make guilty of our disasters the sun, the
moon, and stars; as if we were villains on necessity; fools
by heavenly compulsion; knaves, thieves, and treachers   123
by spherical predominance; drunkards, liars, and adul-   124
terers by an enforced obedience of planetary influence;   125
and all that we are evil in, by a divine thrusting on. An   126
admirable evasion of whoremaster man, to lay his goat-   127

[margin: Edmund knows its not natural]

[handwritten: people think evil things happen to them, when really bad things are done by them...]

100–1 *unstate . . . resolution* give up everything to resolve my doubts   102
presently immediately; *convey* conduct   103 *withal* with the result   104 *late*
recent   105–6 *wisdom . . . thus* natural science can supply various explana-
tions   106–7 *nature . . . effects* humanity ("nature") suffers the consequences
108 *mutinies* rebellions   111 *prediction* ill omen   112 *bias of nature* his natural inclination   114 *hollowness* insincerity   119 *foppery* foolishness   120
surfeits overindulgences   123 *treachers* traitors   124 *spherical predominance*
astrological influence   125 *of* to   126 *thrusting on* enforcement   127 *ad-*
mirable astonishing   127–28 *goatish* lecherous

ish disposition on the charge of a star. My father
129   compounded with my mother under the Dragon's tail,
130   and my nativity was under Ursa Major, so that it follows I am rough and lecherous. Fut! I should have been
that I am, had the maidenliest star in the firmament
twinkled on my bastardizing. Edgar –
    Enter Edgar.
134   and pat he comes, like the catastrophe of the old com-
135   edy. My cue is villainous melancholy, with a sigh like
136   Tom o' Bedlam. – O, these eclipses do portend these
137   divisions. Fa, sol, la, mi.

EDGAR How now, brother Edmund; what serious con-
templation are you in?

140 EDMUND I am thinking, brother, of a prediction I read
this other day, what should follow these eclipses.

EDGAR Do you busy yourself with that?

143 EDMUND I promise you, the effects he writes of succeed
unhappily: [as of unnaturalness between the child and
the parent; death, dearth, dissolutions of ancient ami-
ties; divisions in state, menaces and maledictions against
147 king and nobles; needless diffidences, banishment of
148 friends, dissipation of cohorts, nuptial breaches, and I
know not what.

150 EDGAR How long have you been a sectary astronomical?

EDMUND Come, come,] when saw you my father last?

EDGAR The night gone by.

EDMUND Spake you with him?

EDGAR Ay, two hours together.

---

129 *compounded* had sex **129–30** *Dragon's tail, Ursa Major* the constella-
tions of Draco and the Great Bear **134–35** *catastrophe . . . comedy* conclusion in early comedy (i.e., often arbitrary or unmotivated, but at the
appointed time) **135** *villainous* severe **136** *Tom o' Bedlam* a beggar from
Bedlam (Bethlehem) Hospital, the London madhouse **137** *divisions* (1)
conflicts, (2) musical phrases **143** *succeed* conclude **147** *diffidences* mis-
trust **148** *dissipation of cohorts* disbanding of armies **150** *sectary astronomical* astrological expert

EDMUND   Parted you in good terms? Found you no displeasure in him by word nor countenance? 156
EDGAR   None at all.
EDMUND   Bethink yourself wherein you may have offended him; and at my entreaty forbear his presence
until some little time hath qualified the heat of his dis- 160
pleasure, which at this instant so rageth in him that
with the mischief of your person it would scarcely allay. 162
EDGAR   Some villain hath done me wrong.
EDMUND   That's my fear. I pray you have a continent 164
forbearance till the speed of his rage goes slower; and,
as I say, retire with me to my lodging, from whence I
will fitly bring you to hear my lord speak. Pray ye, go; 167
there's my key. If you do stir abroad, go armed.
EDGAR   Armed, brother?
EDMUND   Brother, I advise you to the best. Go armed. I 170
am no honest man if there be any good meaning
toward you. I have told you what I have seen and
heard; but faintly, nothing like the image and horror of 173
it. Pray you, away.
EDGAR   Shall I hear from you anon?
EDMUND   I do serve you in this business.   *Exit [Edgar].*
A credulous father, and a brother noble,
Whose nature is so far from doing harms
That he suspects none; on whose foolish honesty
My practices ride easy. I see the business. 180
Let me, if not by birth, have lands by wit; 181
All with me's meet that I can fashion fit.   *Exit.* 182

birth vs. worth   *

---

156 *countenance* look   160 *qualified* moderated   162 *the mischief of* injury
to; *allay* be allayed   164 *continent* patient   167 *fitly* when it is appropriate
173–74 *the image . . . it* as horrible as it seemed   180 *practices* plots; *I . . .
business* the plan is now clear   181 *wit* intelligence   182 *with . . . meet* suits
me; *fashion fit* shape to serve my purpose

～ **I.3** *Enter Goneril and Steward [Oswald].*

GONERIL
  Did my father strike my gentleman for chiding of his
    fool?
OSWALD   Ay, madam.
GONERIL
  By day and night he wrongs me. Every hour
4 He flashes into one gross crime or other
  That sets us all at odds. I'll not endure it.
  His knights grow riotous, and himself upbraids us
  On every trifle. When he returns from hunting,
  I will not speak with him. Say I am sick.
9 If you come slack of former services,
10 You shall do well; the fault of it I'll answer.
      [Horns within.]
OSWALD   He's coming, madam; I hear him.
GONERIL
  Put on what weary negligence you please,
13 You and your fellows. I'd have it come to question.
14 If he distaste it, let him to my sister,
  Whose mind and mine I know in that are one,
  [Not to be overruled. Idle old man,
  That still would manage those authorities
  That he hath given away. Now, by my life,
  Old fools are babes again, and must be used
20 With checks as flatteries, when they are seen abused.]
  Remember what I have said.
OSWALD   Well, madam.
GONERIL
  And let his knights have colder looks among you.
  What grows of it, no matter; advise your fellows so.

I.3 Albany's castle   4 *crime* offense   9 *come . . . services* serve him less well
than usual   10 *answer* answer for   13 *come . . . question* made an issue   14
distaste dislike   20 *checks . . . flatteries* rebukes as well as compliments;
they . . . seen the compliments are

[I would breed from hence occasions, and I shall,   25
That I may speak.] I'll write straight to my sister   26
To hold my course. Prepare for dinner.   *Exeunt.*   27

*

∽ **I.4** *Enter Kent [disguised].*

KENT
   If but as well I other accents borrow   1
   That can my speech defuse, my (good intent)   2
   May carry through itself to that full issue   3
   For which I razed my likeness. Now, banished Kent,   4
   If thou canst serve where thou dost stand condemned,
   So may it come thy master whom thou (lov'st)   6
   Shall find thee full of labors.   7
         Horns within. Enter Lear, [Knight,] and Attendants.   *doesn't think*
LEAR   Let me not stay a jot for dinner; go get it ready.   8 *he's lost*
         [Exit an Attendant.] How now, what art thou?   9 *power*
KENT   A man, sir.   10
LEAR   What dost thou profess? What wouldst thou with   11
   us?
KENT   I do profess to be no less than I seem, to serve him
   truly that will put me in trust, to love him that is honest, to converse with him that is wise and says little, to   15
   fear judgment, to fight when I cannot choose, and to   16
   eat no fish.   17
LEAR   What art thou?   └→ *only disguising*
                                  his appearance

---

25 *breed . . . occasions* use this to provoke scenes   26 *speak* speak my mind
27 *hold . . . course* pursue the same course I do

   I.4 1 *If . . . borrow* i.e., if I disguise my voice as effectively as I do my appearance 2 *defuse* confuse, disguise 3 *issue* outcome 4 *razed . . . likeness*
erased my appearance (including "razoring" his beard) 6 *come* happen that
7 *full . . . labors* i.e., hard at work 7 s.d. *Horns within* hunting horns offstage
8 *stay* wait 9 *what* who 11 *dost . . . profess* is your trade 15 *converse* asso-
ciate 16 *fear judgment* show respect for authority; *choose* avoid it 17 *eat no
fish* (a joke whose point has obviously been lost: not to be Catholic and thus
forbidden to eat meat on Fridays? to be a meat-eater only – i.e., manly?)

KENT   A very honest-hearted fellow, and as poor as the
20   king.
LEAR   If thou be'st as poor for a subject as he's for a king,
thou art poor enough. What wouldst thou?
KENT   Service.
LEAR   Who wouldst thou serve?
KENT   You.
LEAR   Dost thou know me, fellow?
KENT   No, sir, but you have that in your countenance
28   which I would fain call master.
LEAR   What's that?
30   KENT   Authority.   *honesty*
LEAR   What services canst thou do?
32   KENT   I can keep honest counsel, ride, run, mar a curious tale in telling it, and deliver a plain message
bluntly. That which ordinary men are fit for I am qualified in, and the best of me is diligence.
LEAR   How old art thou?
KENT   Not so young, sir, to love a woman for singing,
nor so old to dote on her for anything. I have years on
my back forty-eight.
40   LEAR   Follow me; thou shalt serve me. If I like thee no
worse after dinner, I will not part from thee yet. Din-
42   ner, ho, dinner! Where's my knave? my fool? Go you
and call my fool hither.   *[Exit an Attendant.]*
   Enter Steward [Oswald].
You, you, sirrah, where's my daughter?
OSWALD   So please you –
                                            Exit.
46   LEAR   What says the fellow there? Call the clotpoll back.
[Exit Knight.] Where's my fool? Ho, I think the world 's
asleep. *[Enter Knight.]* How now? Where's that mongrel?

---

28 *fain* like to   **32** *keep . . . counsel* respect confidences   **32–33** *curious*
complicated   **42** *knave* boy (the term could be affectionate)   **46** *clotpoll*
blockhead

KNIGHT   He says, my lord, your daughter is not well.   *50*

LEAR   Why came not the slave back to me when I called
him?

KNIGHT   Sir, he answered me in the roundest manner, he   *53*
would not.

LEAR   He would not?

KNIGHT   My lord, I know not what the matter is; but to
my judgment your highness is not entertained with   *57*
that ceremonious affection as you were wont. There's a   *58*
great abatement of kindness appears as well in the gen-   *59*
eral dependents as in the duke himself also and your   *60*
daughter.

LEAR   Ha? Say'st thou so?

KNIGHT   I beseech you pardon me, my lord, if I be mis-
taken; for my duty cannot be silent when I think your
highness wronged.

LEAR   Thou but rememb'rest me of mine own concep-   *66*
tion. I have perceived a most faint neglect of late,
which I have rather blamed as mine own jealous curios-   *68*
ity than as a very pretense and purpose of unkindness. I   *69*
will look further into't. But where's my fool? I have not   *70*
seen him this two days.

KNIGHT   Since my young lady's going into France, sir,
the fool hath much pined away.

LEAR   No more of that; I have noted it well. Go you and
tell my daughter I would speak with her. *[Exit Knight.]*
Go you, call hither my fool.   *[Exit an Attendant.]*
   Enter Steward [Oswald].
O, you, sir, you! Come you hither, sir. Who am I, sir?

OSWALD   My lady's father.

LEAR   "My lady's father"? My lord's knave, you whoreson
dog, you slave, you cur!   *80*

---

53 *roundest* rudest   57 *entertained* treated   58 *wont* accustomed to   **59–60**
the . . . dependents all the servants   **66** *rememb'rest* remind   **66–67** *concep-
tion* perception   **68** *jealous curiosity* hypersensitiveness   **69** *very pretense* real
intention

OSWALD   I am none of these, my lord; I beseech your
pardon.

LEAR   Do you bandy looks with me, you rascal?
   [Strikes him.]

OSWALD   I'll not be strucken, my lord.

85   KENT   Nor tripped neither, you base football player.
   [Trips up his heels.]

LEAR   I thank thee, fellow. Thou serv'st me, and I'll love
thee.

88   KENT   Come, sir, arise, away. I'll teach you differences.
89   Away, away. If you will measure your lubber's length
90   again, tarry; but away. Go to! Have you wisdom? So.
   [Pushes him out.]

LEAR   Now, my friendly knave, I thank thee. There's
92   earnest of thy service.
   [Gives money.] Enter Fool.

93   FOOL   Let me hire him too. Here's my coxcomb.
   [Offers Kent his cap.]

LEAR   How now, my pretty knave? How dost thou?

FOOL   Sirrah, you were best take my coxcomb.

KENT   Why, fool?

FOOL   Why? For taking one's part that's out of favor.
98   Nay, an thou canst not smile as the wind sits, thou'lt
catch cold shortly. There, take my coxcomb. Why, this
100   fellow has banished two on's daughters, and did the
third a blessing against his will. If thou follow him,
thou must needs wear my coxcomb. – How now,
103   nuncle? Would I had two coxcombs and two daughters.

LEAR   Why, my boy?

---

85 *football player* (football was a lower-class street game)   88 *differences* dis-
tinctions of rank   89 *measure . . . length* i.e., have me trip you up again; *lubber* oaf   92 *earnest of* a down payment on   93 *coxcomb* fool's cap   98 *an* if
98–99 *an . . . shortly* if you can't please those in power, you'll soon be out in
the cold   100 *banished* as Kent says, "Freedom lives hence, and banishment
is here" (I.1.186); *on's* of his   103 *nuncle* (mine) uncle

FOOL   If I gave them all my living, I'd keep my coxcombs   105
myself. There's mine; beg another of thy daughters.

LEAR   Take heed, sirrah – the whip.

FOOL   Truth's a dog must to kennel; he must be whipped
out, when the Lady Brach may stand by th' fire and   109
stink.

LEAR   A pestilent gall to me.   111

FOOL   Sirrah, I'll teach thee a speech.

LEAR   Do.

FOOL   Mark it, nuncle.

> Have more than thou showest,
> Speak less than thou knowest,
> Lend less than thou owest,   117
> Ride more than thou goest,   118
> Learn more than thou trowest,   119
> Set less than thou throwest;   120
> Leave thy drink and thy whore,
> And keep in-a-door,
> And thou shalt have more
> Than two tens to a score.   124

KENT   This is nothing, fool.

FOOL   Then 'tis like the breath of an unfee'd lawyer – 126
you gave me nothing for't. Can you make no use of
nothing, nuncle?

LEAR   Why, no, boy. Nothing can be made out of nothing.   130

FOOL   *[To Kent]* Prithee tell him, so much the rent of his   131
land comes to; he will not believe a fool.

---

105 *living* possessions   105–6 *I'd ... myself* I'd be a double fool   109 *out*
out of doors   109–10 *when ... stink* brach = bitch; as Goneril and Regan are
favored and the truthful Cordelia exiled   111 *gall* bitterness, sore   117
owest own   118 *goest* walk   119 *trowest* believe (i.e., don't believe everything
you hear)   120 *Set ... throwest* bet less than you win (at dice)   124 *score*
twenty (i.e., you'll do better than break even)   126 *breath* speech; *unfee'd* un-
paid (lawyers proverbially will not plead without a fee)   131–32 *so ... to*
i.e., he no longer has any land, and therefore no income from it

LEAR   A bitter fool.

FOOL   Dost thou know the difference, my boy, between
a bitter fool and a sweet one?

LEAR   No, lad; teach me.

FOOL   [That lord that counseled thee
                   To give away thy land,
                   Come place him here by me –
140   Do thou for him stand.
                   The sweet and bitter fool
142   Will presently appear;
143   The one in motley here,
                   The other found out there.

LEAR   Dost thou call me fool, boy?

FOOL   <u>All thy other titles thou hast given away; that thou
wast born with.</u>

KENT   This is not altogether fool, my lord.

149 FOOL   No, faith; lords and great men will not let me. If I
had a monopoly out, they would have part on't. And
ladies too, they will not let me have all the fool to myself; they'll be snatching.] Nuncle, give me an egg, and
I'll give thee two crowns.

LEAR   What two crowns shall they be?

FOOL   Why, after I have cut the egg i' th' middle and eat
156 up the meat, the two crowns of the egg. When thou
clovest thy crown i' th' middle and gav'st away both
parts, thou bor'st thine ass on thy back o'er the dirt.
Thou hadst little wit in thy bald crown when thou
160 gav'st thy golden one away. If I speak like myself in this,
161 let him be whipped that first finds it so.

162 [Sings.]   Fools had ne'er less grace in a year,
163   For wise men are grown foppish,

---

142 *Will . . . appear* i.e., it will be immediately apparent which is which
143 *motley* the jester's particolored costume   149 *let me* i.e., let me have all
the foolishness, be "altogether fool"   156 *two . . . egg* i.e., the empty shell
160 *like myself* i.e., like a fool   161 *that . . . so* i.e., for being a fool himself
162 *had . . . year* are now out of fashion   163 *foppish* foolish

         And know not how their wits to wear,   164
             Their manners are so apish.   165

LEAR   When were you wont to be so full of songs, sirrah? 166

FOOL   I have used it, nuncle, e'er since thou mad'st thy daughters thy mothers; for when thou gav'st them the rod, and put'st down thine own breeches,

    [Sings.] Then they for sudden joy did weep,   *170*
            And I for sorrow sung,
         That such a king should play bopeep   172
            And go the fools among.

Prithee, nuncle, keep a schoolmaster that can teach thy fool to lie. I would fain learn to lie.   175

LEAR   An you lie, sirrah, we'll have you whipped. 176

FOOL   I marvel what kin thou and thy daughters are. They'll have me whipped for speaking true; thou'lt have me whipped for lying; and sometimes I am whipped for holding my peace. I had rather be any *180* kind o' thing than a fool, and yet I would not be thee, nuncle; thou hast pared thy wit o' both sides and left nothing i' th' middle. Here comes one o' the parings.

    Enter Goneril.

LEAR   How now, daughter? What makes that frontlet on? 184 You are too much of late i' th' frown.

FOOL   Thou wast a pretty fellow when thou hadst no need to care for her frowning. Now thou art an O with- 187 out a figure. I am better than thou art now: I am a fool, thou art nothing. *[To Goneril]* Yes, forsooth, I will hold my tongue. So your face bids me, though you say noth- *190* ing. Mum, mum,
         He that keeps nor crust nor crumb,
         Weary of all, shall want some. –

---

164 *their . . . wear* to use their heads   165 *apish* both stupid and imitative **166** *wont* accustomed   172 *play bopeep* i.e., act like a child   175 *fain* gladly **176** *An* if   **184** *What . . . on* why are you wearing such a face (frontlet = forehead or a headband worn on it)   187–88 *an . . . figure* a zero with no number in front of it (i.e., nothing)

[Points at Lear.]

194   That's a shelled peasecod.

GONERIL

195   Not only, sir, this your all-licensed fool,
       But other of your insolent retinue
       Do hourly carp and quarrel, breaking forth
198   In rank and not-to-be-endurèd riots. Sir,
       I had thought by making this well known unto you
200   To have found a safe redress, but now grow fearful,
201   By what yourself too late have spoke and done,
202   That you protect this course, and put it on
       By your allowance; which if you should, the fault
204   Would not scape censure, nor the redresses sleep,
205   Which, in the tender of a wholesome weal,
206   Might in their working do you that offense,
       Which else were shame, that then necessity
       Will call discreet proceeding.

FOOL   For you know, nuncle,

210   The hedge-sparrow fed the cuckoo so long ⎤
            That it's had it head bit off by it young. ⎦

212   So out went the candle, and we were left darkling.

LEAR   Are you our daughter?

GONERIL

       I would you would make use of your good wisdom
215   (Whereof I know you are fraught) and put away
216   These dispositions which of late transport you
       From what you rightly are.

---

194 *shelled peasecod* empty pea pod   195 *all-licensed* allowed to do anything
198 *rank* gross   200 *safe redress* sure remedy   201 *too late* lately   202
put . . . on encourage it   204 *redresses sleep* punishment lie dormant   205
tender . . . weal government of a healthy commonwealth   206–8 *Might . . .
proceeding* might humiliate you, but, being necessary, would be merely prudent; necessity = what the situation demands   210–11 *The . . . young* (the
cuckoo lays its eggs in other birds' nests; the young cuckoos eventually destroy the sparrow that has been feeding them); *it . . . it* its . . . its   212 *darkling* in darkness   215 *fraught* full   216 *dispositions* moods

FOOL   May not an ass know when the cart draws the
horse? Whoop, Jug, I love thee!   219
LEAR
Does any here know me? This is not Lear.   220
Does Lear walk thus? speak thus? Where are his eyes?
Either his notion weakens, his discernings   222
Are lethargied – Ha! Waking? 'Tis not so.   223
Who is it that can tell me who I am?
FOOL   Lear's shadow.
[LEAR
I would learn that; for, by the marks of sovereignty,
Knowledge, and reason, I should be false persuaded
I had daughters.
FOOL   Which they will make an obedient father.]
LEAR   Your name, fair gentlewoman?   230
GONERIL
This admiration, sir, is much o' th' savor   231
Of other your new pranks. I do beseech you
To understand my purposes aright.
As you are old and reverend, should be wise.
Here do you keep a hundred knights and squires,
Men so disordered, so debauched and bold   236
That this our court, infected with their manners,
Shows like a riotous inn. Epicurism and lust   238
Makes it more like a tavern or a brothel
Than a graced palace. The shame itself doth speak   240
For instant remedy. Be then desired
By her that else will take the things she begs
A little to disquantity your train,   243
And the remainders that shall still depend   244

---

219 *Jug* Joan, generic name for a whore **222** *notion* mind; *discernings* perceptions **223** *Waking?* am I awake? **231** *admiration* spectacle (something to be wondered at) **236** *bold* impudent **238** *Shows* looks; *Epicurism* gluttony **240** *graced* dignified **243** *disquantity . . . train* reduce the size of your retinue **244** *depend* be your dependents

245   To be such men as may besort your age,
    Which know themselves, and you.
LEAR   Darkness and devils!
247   Saddle my horses; call my train together.
    Degenerate bastard, I'll not trouble thee:
    Yet have I left a daughter.
GONERIL
250   You strike my people, and your disordered rabble
    Make servants of their betters.
       Enter Albany.
LEAR
    Woe that too late repents. – [O, sir, are you come?]
    Is it your will? Speak, sir. – Prepare my horses.
    Ingratitude! thou marble-hearted fiend,
    More hideous when thou show'st thee in a child
    Than the sea monster.
ALBANY   Pray, sir, be patient.
LEAR
258   Detested kite, thou liest.
259   My train are men of choice and rarest parts,
260   That all particulars of duty know
261   And in the most exact regard support
262   The worships of their name. O most small fault,
    How ugly didst thou in Cordelia show!
264   Which, like an engine, wrenched my frame of nature
    From the fixed place; drew from my heart all love
    And added to the gall. O Lear, Lear, Lear!
267   Beat at this gate that let thy folly in
      [Strikes his head.]
    And thy dear judgment out. Go, go, my people.

---

245 *besort* befit   **247** *Saddle . . . together* (Most editors send some knights off to do Lear's bidding, but it is more likely that everyone is immobilized with astonishment: he has to order the horses saddled again at line 253.) **258** *Detested kite* detestable bird of prey   **259** *parts* qualities   **261** *in . . . regard* with the most scrupulous attention   **262** *worships* honor   **264** *engine* machine   **264–265** *my . . . place* the structure of my being from its foundations   **267** *this gate* presumably his head

ALBANY
  My lord, I am guiltless, as I am ignorant
  Of what hath moved you.   270
LEAR   It may be so, my lord.
  Hear, Nature, hear; dear goddess, hear:
  Suspend thy purpose if thou didst intend
  To make this creature fruitful.
  Into her womb convey sterility,
  Dry up in her the organs of increase,
  And from her derogate body never spring   276
  A babe to honor her. If she must teem,   277
  Create her child of spleen, that it may live   278
  And be a thwart disnatured torment to her.   279
  Let it stamp wrinkles in her brow of youth,   280
  With cadent tears fret channels in her cheeks,   281
  Turn all her mother's pains and benefits   282
  To laughter and contempt, that she may feel
  How sharper than a serpent's tooth it is
  To have a thankless child. Away, away!   *Exit.*   285
ALBANY
  Now, gods that we adore, whereof comes this?
GONERIL
  Never afflict yourself to know more of it,
  But let his disposition have that scope   288
  As dotage gives it.
     Enter Lear.
LEAR
  What, fifty of my followers at a clap?   290
  Within a fortnight?
ALBANY   What's the matter, sir?
LEAR
  I'll tell thee. *[To Goneril]* Life and death, I am ashamed
  That thou hast power to shake my manhood thus!

---

276 *derogate* debased   277 *teem* breed   278 *spleen* malice   279 *thwart disnatured* perverse, unnatural   281 *cadent* falling; *fret* wear   282 *pains* care
285 **s.d.** The fool apparently remains onstage.   288 *disposition* mood

294 That these hot tears, which break from me perforce,
Should make thee worth them. Blasts and fogs upon
thee!
296 Th' untented woundings of a father's curse
297 Pierce every sense about thee! Old fond eyes,
298 Beweep this cause again I'll pluck ye out
299 And cast you, with the waters that you loose,
300 To temper clay. [Yea, is it come to this?]
Ha! Let it be so. I have another daughter,
302 Who I am sure is kind and comfortable.
When she shall hear this of thee, with her nails
She'll flay thy wolvish visage. Thou shalt find
That I'll resume the shape which thou dost think
I have cast off forever.

Exit [Lear with Kent and Attendants].

GONERIL   Do you mark that?

ALBANY
308 I cannot be so partial, Goneril,
To the great love I bear you –

GONERIL
310 Pray you, content. – What, Oswald, ho!
[To Fool]
You, sir, more knave than fool, after your master!

FOOL   Nuncle Lear, nuncle Lear, tarry. Take the fool with
thee.

A fox, when one has caught her,
And such a daughter,
316 Should sure to the slaughter,
317 If my cap would buy a halter.
So the fool follows after.   _Exit._

GONERIL
This man hath had good counsel – a hundred knights!

_____

294 _perforce_ i.e., against my will   296 _untented woundings_ wounds too deep
to be probed   297 _fond_ foolish   298 _Beweep_ if you weep over   299 _loose_ let
loose   300 _temper_ soften   302 _comfortable_ comforting   308–9 _partial . . ._
_To_ biased . . . by   316 _sure_ surely be sent   317 _halter_ noose

'Tis politic and safe to let him keep   320
At point a hundred knights – yes, that on every dream,   321
Each buzz, each fancy, each complaint, dislike,   322
He may enguard his dotage with their pow'rs   323
And hold our lives in mercy. – Oswald, I say!   324

ALBANY
Well, you may fear too far.

GONERIL
Safer than trust too far.
Let me still take away the harms I fear,
Not fear still to be taken. I know his heart.
What he hath uttered I have writ my sister.
If she sustain him and his hundred knights,   *330*
When I have showed th' unfitness –
        Enter Steward [Oswald].   How now, Oswald?
What, have you writ that letter to my sister?

OSWALD   Ay, madam.

GONERIL
Take you some company, and away to horse.
Inform her full of my particular fear,
And thereto add such reasons of your own
As may compact it more. Get you gone,   337
And hasten your return. *[Exit Oswald.]* No, no, my lord,
This milky gentleness and course of yours,   339
Though I condemn not, yet under pardon,   340
You are much more ataskéd for want of wisdom   341
Than praised for harmful mildness.

ALBANY
How far your eyes may pierce I cannot tell;
Striving to better, oft we mar what's well.

GONERIL   Nay then –

ALBANY   Well, well; th' event.   *Exeunt.*   346

*

---

320 *politic* prudent   321 *At point* armed   322 *buzz* murmur, whim   323
enguard safeguard   324 *in mercy* at his mercy   337 *compact* confirm   339
milky . . . course mild and gentle way   340 *under pardon* if you'll pardon me
341 *ataskéd* taken to task   346 *th' event* let's await the outcome

⌘ **I.5** *Enter Lear, Kent [disguised], and Fool.*

1 LEAR   Go you before to Gloucester with these letters. Acquaint my daughter no further with anything you
3 know than comes from her demand out of the letter. If
your diligence be not speedy, I shall be there afore you.
KENT   I will not sleep, my lord, till I have delivered your
letter.   *Exit.*
FOOL   If a man's brains were in's heels, were't not in dan-
8 ger of kibes?
LEAR   Ay, boy.
10 FOOL   Then I prithee be merry. Thy wit shall not go slipshod.
LEAR   Ha, ha, ha.
13 FOOL   Shalt see thy other daughter will use thee kindly;
14 for though she's as like this as a crab's like an apple, yet
I can tell what I can tell.
LEAR   What canst tell, boy?
FOOL   She will taste as like this as a crab does to a crab.
18 Thou canst tell why one's nose stands i' th' middle on's
face?
20 LEAR   No.
FOOL   Why, to keep one's eyes of either side's nose, that
what a man cannot smell out he may spy into.
23 LEAR   I did her wrong.   *realization*
FOOL   Canst tell how an oyster makes his shell?
LEAR   No.
FOOL   Nor I neither; but I can tell why a snail has a
house.

I.5   1 *before* ahead of me; *Gloucester* (apparently not the earl but the town,
which would therefore be the location of Regan and Cornwall's castle); *these
letters* this letter (i.e., the letters that comprise one message; cf. "these words")
3 *demand . . . of* questions prompted by   **8** *kibes* chilblains   **10–11** *shall . . .
slipshod* will not have to wear slippers because of chilblains (the point is that
feet with brains would not make this journey)   **13** *Shalt* thou shalt; *kindly*
both affectionately and after her kind – i.e., in the same way   **14** *crab*
crabapple, proverbially sour   **18** *on's* of his   **23** *her* Cordelia

LEAR Why?

FOOL Why, to put's head in; not to give it away to his
daughters, and leave his horns without a case.   30

LEAR I will forget my nature. So kind a father! – Be my 31
horses ready?

FOOL Thy asses are gone about 'em. The reason why the 33
seven stars are no more than seven is a pretty reason.

LEAR Because they are not eight.

FOOL Yes indeed. Thou wouldst make a good fool.

LEAR To take't again perforce – Monster ingratitude! 37

FOOL If thou wert my fool, nuncle, I'd have thee beaten
for being old before thy time.

LEAR How's that?   40

FOOL Thou shouldst not have been old till thou hadst
been wise.

LEAR
    O, let me not be mad, not mad, sweet heaven!
    Keep me in temper; I would not be mad!   44
        [Enter a Gentleman.]
    How now, are the horses ready?

GENTLEMAN Ready, my lord.

LEAR Come, boy.

FOOL
    She that's a maid now, and laughs at my departure, 48
    Shall not be a maid long, unless things be cut shorter.
                                            Exeunt.

                        *

---

30 *horns* (with a quibble on the cuckold's horns, implying that Goneril and
Regan are illegitimate) **31** *nature* paternal instincts **33–34** *the seven stars*
the constellation the Pleiades **37** *To . . . perforce* to take it back forcibly
(Lear either rages at Goneril's revocation of his privileges or contemplates re-
asserting his power) **44** *in temper* temperate, sane **48–49** *She . . . shorter*
i.e., the maid who laughed at my leaving would be a fool and would not remain a virgin unless men were castrated

∾ **II.1** *Enter Bastard [Edmund] and Curan severally.*

1 EDMUND   Save thee, Curan.

CURAN   And you, sir. I have been with your father, and given him notice that the Duke of Cornwall and Regan his duchess will be here with him this night.

EDMUND   How comes that?

CURAN   Nay, I know not. You have heard of the news abroad – I mean the whispered ones, for they are yet
8   but ear-kissing arguments?

EDMUND   Not I. Pray you, what are they?

10 CURAN   Have you heard of no likely wars toward, 'twixt the Dukes of Cornwall and Albany?

EDMUND   Not a word.

CURAN   You may do, then, in time. Fare you well, sir.

                       Exit.

EDMUND
14   The duke be here tonight? The better best!
15   This weaves itself perforce into my business.
  My father hath set guard to take my brother,
17   And I have one thing of a queasy question
18   Which I must act. Briefness and fortune, work!
19   – Brother, a word: descend. Brother, I say!
  Enter Edgar.
20   My father watches. O sir, fly this place.
21   Intelligence is given where you are hid.
  You have now the good advantage of the night.
  Have you not spoken 'gainst the Duke of Cornwall?
  He's coming hither; now i' th' night, i' th' haste,
  And Regan with him. Have you nothing said

II.1 Gloucester's house **s.d.** *severally* separately   1 *Save thee* God save thee (a casual greeting like "good day")   8 *ear-kissing arguments* whispered matters   10 *toward* impending   14 *better best* very best   15 *perforce* necessarily   17 *queasy question* delicate problem   18 *Briefness . . . work* may speed and luck work for me   19 *descend* (possibly Edgar has appeared on the upper-stage gallery)   21 *Intelligence* information

Upon his party 'gainst the Duke of Albany?   26
Advise yourself.   27
EDGAR   I am sure on't, not a word.
EDMUND
I hear my father coming. Pardon me:
In cunning I must draw my sword upon you.
Draw, seem to defend yourself; now quit you well. –   30
Yield! Come before my father! Light ho, here! –
Fly, brother. – Torches, torches! – So farewell.

         Exit Edgar.

Some blood drawn on me would beget opinion   33
Of my more fierce endeavor.
 [Wounds his arm.]   I have seen drunkards
Do more than this in sport. – Father, father!
Stop, stop! No help?
 Enter Gloucester, and Servants with torches.
GLOUCESTER
Now, Edmund, where's the villain?
EDMUND
Here stood he in the dark, his sharp sword out,
Mumbling of wicked charms, conjuring the moon
To stand auspicious mistress.   40
GLOUCESTER   But where is he?
EDMUND
Look, sir, I bleed.
GLOUCESTER   Where is the villain, Edmund?
EDMUND
Fled this way, sir, when by no means he could –
GLOUCESTER
Pursue him, ho! Go after.   *[Exeunt some Servants.]*
      By no means what?
EDMUND
Persuade me to the murder of your lordship;

---

26 *Upon . . . 'gainst* relating to his quarrel with   27 *Advise yourself* think
about it; *on't* of it   30 *quit you* acquit yourself   33–34 *beget . . . endeavor*
give the impression that I fought fiercely   40 *stand* act as his

45 But that I told him the revenging gods
46 'Gainst parricides did all the thunder bend;
     Spoke with how manifold and strong a bond
48 The child was bound to th' father – sir, in fine,
49 Seeing how loathly opposite I stood
50 To his unnatural purpose, in fell motion
51 With his preparèd sword he charges home
52 My unprovided body, latched mine arm;
53 And when he saw my best alarumed spirits
54 Bold in the quarrel's right, roused to th' encounter,
55 Or whether ghasted by the noise I made,
     Full suddenly he fled.

GLOUCESTER   Let him fly far.
     Not in this land shall he remain uncaught;
58 And found – dispatch. The noble duke my master,
59 My worthy arch and patron, comes tonight:
60 By his authority I will proclaim it
     That he which finds him shall deserve our thanks,
     Bringing the murderous coward to the stake;
     He that conceals him, death.

EDMUND
     When I dissuaded him from his intent
65 And found him pight to do it, with curst speech
66 I threatened to discover him. He replied,
67 "Thou unpossessing bastard, dost thou think,
68 If I would stand against thee, would the reposal
     Of any trust, virtue, or worth in thee
70 Make thy words faithed? No. What I should deny

---

45 *But that* however   46 *thunder bend* thunderbolts aim   48 *in fine* finally
49 *loathly opposite* loathingly opposed   50 *fell motion* deadly action   51
charges home thrusts directly at   52 *unprovided* unprotected; *latched* hit   53
best alarumed fully aroused   54 *quarrel's right* justice of the cause   55
ghasted frightened   58 *found – dispatch* once found – death   59 *arch . . .
patron* chief patron   65 *pight* determined; *curst* angry   66 *discover* expose
67 *unpossessing* unpropertied, landless   68 *reposal* placing   70 *faithed* believed; *What . . . should* whatever I would

(As this I would, ay, though thou didst produce
My very character) I'd turn it all   72
To thy suggestion, plot, and damnèd practice;   73
And thou must make a dullard of the world,   74
If they not thought the profits of my death
Were very pregnant and potential spirits   76
To make thee seek it."   77

GLOUCESTER   O strange and fastened villain!
Would he deny his letter, said he? [I never got him.]   78
    Tucket within.
Hark, the duke's trumpets. I know not why he comes.
All ports I'll bar; the villain shall not scape;   80
The duke must grant me that. Besides, his picture
I will send far and near, that all the kingdom
May have due note of him; and of my land,
Loyal and natural boy, I'll work the means
To make thee capable.   85
    Enter Cornwall, Regan, and Attendants.

CORNWALL
How now, my noble friend? Since I came hither
(Which I can call but now) I have heard strange news.   87

REGAN
If it be true, all vengeance comes too short
Which can pursue th' offender. How dost, my lord?

GLOUCESTER
O madam, my old heart is cracked, it's cracked.   *90*

REGAN
What, did my father's godson seek your life?
He whom my father named, your Edgar?

GLOUCESTER
O lady, lady, shame would have it hid.

---

72 *character* handwriting – i.e., evidence in my own hand; *turn* ascribe   73
practice evil schemes   74 *make . . . world* consider everyone stupid   76 *preg-nant . . . spirits* meaningful and powerful motives   77 *strange . . . fastened*
unnatural and hardened   78 *got* fathered   **s.d.** *Tucket* trumpet signal   80
ports both seaports and town gates   85 *capable* legally able to inherit   87
call but say was only

REGAN
Was he not companion with the riotous knights
That tended upon my father?
GLOUCESTER
I know not, madam. 'Tis too bad, too bad.
EDMUND
Yes, madam, he was of that consort.
REGAN
98   No marvel then though he were ill affected.
99   'Tis they have put him on the old man's death,
100   To have th' expense and waste of his revenues.
I have this present evening from my sister
Been well informed of them, and with such cautions
That, if they come to sojourn at my house,
I'll not be there.
CORNWALL   Nor I, assure thee, Regan.
Edmund, I hear that you have shown your father
A childlike office.
EDMUND   It was my duty, sir.
GLOUCESTER
107   He did bewray his practice, and received
This hurt you see, striving to apprehend him.
CORNWALL
Is he pursued?
GLOUCESTER   Ay, my good lord.
CORNWALL
110   If he be taken, he shall never more
111   Be feared of doing harm. Make your own purpose,
How in my strength you please. For you, Edmund,
Whose virtue and obedience doth this instant
So much commend itself, you shall be ours.
Natures of such deep trust we shall much need;
You we first seize on.

---

98 *though* that; *ill affected* disposed to evil   **99** *put* set   **100** *waste* plunder
107 *bewray . . . practice* expose Edgar's plot   **111–12** *Make . . . please* carry
out your intentions making what use you wish of my powers

EDMUND   I shall serve you, sir,
  Truly, however else.   117
GLOUCESTER   For him I thank your grace.
CORNWALL
  You know not why we came to visit you?
REGAN
  Thus out of season, threading dark-eyed night.   120
  Occasions, noble Gloucester, of some prize,   121
  Wherein we must have use of your advice.
  Our father he hath writ, so hath our sister,
  Of differences, which I best thought it fit   124
  To answer from our home. The several messengers   125
  From hence attend dispatch. Our good old friend,   126
  Lay comforts to your bosom, and bestow
  Your needful counsel to our businesses,   128
  Which craves the instant use.   129
GLOUCESTER   I serve you, madam.
  Your graces are right welcome.   *Exeunt. Flourish.* 130

                          *

∾ **II.2** *Enter Kent [disguised] and Steward [Oswald],
  severally.*

OSWALD   Good dawning to thee, friend. Art of this house? 1
KENT   Ay.   2
OSWALD   Where may we set our horses?
KENT   I' th' mire.
OSWALD   Prithee, if thou lov'st me, tell me.   5
KENT   I love thee not.
OSWALD   Why then, I care not for thee.

----

117 *however else* if nothing else   120 *out of season* untimely (i.e., traveling at
night) 121 *prize* price, importance 124 *differences* quarrels 125
answer . . . home deal with away from home; *several* various 126 *attend*
await 128 *needful* needed 129 *the . . . use* immediate action
  II.2 1 *Art of* are you a servant in   2 *Ay* (since the house is Gloucester's,
Kent is lying, presumably as a way of picking a fight with Oswald)   5 *if . . .
me* i.e., be kind enough to

8   KENT   If I had thee in Lipsbury Pinfold, I would make thee care for me.

10   OSWALD   Why dost thou use me thus? I know thee not.

KENT   Fellow, I know thee.

OSWALD   What dost thou know me for?

13   KENT   A knave, a rascal, an eater of broken meats; a base,
14   proud, shallow, beggarly, three-suited, hundred-pound,
15   filthy worsted-stocking knave; a lily-livered, action-
16   taking, whoreson, glass-gazing, superserviceable, finical
17   rogue; one-trunk-inheriting slave; one that wouldst be
  a bawd in way of good service, and art nothing but the
19   composition of a knave, beggar, coward, pander, and
20   the son and heir of a mongrel bitch; one whom I will
  beat into clamorous whining if thou deny'st the least
22   syllable of thy addition.

OSWALD   Why, what a monstrous fellow art thou, thus to rail on one that is neither known of thee nor knows thee!

26   KENT   What a brazen-faced varlet art thou to deny thou knowest me! Is it two days ago since I tripped up thy heels and beat thee before the king? *[Draws his sword.]* Draw, you rogue, for though it be night, yet the moon
30   shines. I'll make a sop o' th' moonshine of you. You
31   whoreson cullionly barbermonger, draw!

---

8 *Lipsbury Pinfold* in the pen of my lips – i.e., between my teeth (jocularly, as a place name)   10 *use* treat   13 *broken meats* leftover food, fit for menials 14 *three-suited* (male household servants were furnished with three suits per year: Kent attacks Oswald's pretensions to gentility); *hundred-pound* the minimum annual income for a gentleman   15 *worsted-stocking* coarse wool stocking (a gentleman would wear silk); *lily-livered* cowardly; *action-taking* litigious (resorting to legal action instead of fighting)   16 *glass-gazing . . . finical* vain, toadying, fussy   17 *one-trunk-inheriting* owning no more than will fit in a single trunk   17–18 *a bawd . . . service* a pimp if asked   19 *composition* composite   22 *addition* title (i.e., the names I have just called you) 26 *varlet* rogue   30 *make . . . moonshine* fill you with holes so your body will sop up moonshine   31 *cullionly* despicable (cullions are testicles; the insult is analogous to calling someone a prick); *barbermonger* (a particularly inventive insult: on the model of whoremonger, a pimp for barbers, one who supplies them with clients, hence who caters to the needs of effeminate men)

OSWALD   Away, I have nothing to do with thee.

KENT   Draw, you rascal. You come with letters against the
king, and take Vanity the puppet's part against the roy-   34
alty of her father. Draw, you rogue, or I'll so carbonado   35
your shanks. Draw, you rascal. Come your ways!   36

OSWALD   Help, ho! Murder! Help!

KENT   Strike, you slave! Stand, rogue! Stand, you neat   38
slave! Strike!
  [Beats him.]

OSWALD   Help, ho! Murder, murder!   40
  Enter Bastard [Edmund, with his rapier drawn],
  Cornwall, Regan, Gloucester, Servants.

EDMUND   How now? What's the matter? Part!

KENT   With you, goodman boy, if you please! Come, I'll   42
flesh ye; come on, young master.   43

GLOUCESTER   Weapons? Arms? What's the matter here?

CORNWALL   Keep peace, upon your lives. He dies that
strikes again. What is the matter?

REGAN   The messengers from our sister and the king.

CORNWALL   What is your difference? Speak.   48

OSWALD   I am scarce in breath, my lord.

KENT   No marvel, you have so bestirred your valor. You   50
cowardly rascal, nature disclaims in thee. A tailor made   51
thee.

CORNWALL   Thou art a strange fellow. A tailor make a
man?

KENT   A tailor, sir. A stonecutter or a painter could not
have made him so ill, though they had been but two   56
years o' th' trade.   57

CORNWALL
  Speak yet, how grew your quarrel?

---

34 *take . . . part* (support the vain, overdressed Goneril)   35 *carbonado* slash
36 *come . . . ways* come on, get to it   38 *neat* prissy   42 *goodman boy* (both
are deliberate insults to Edmund as a gentleman: goodman = yeoman or
farmer)   43 *flesh ye* give you your first taste of blood   48 *difference* quarrel
51 *disclaims in* disowns   56 *ill* badly   57 *o' th'* at the

OSWALD This ancient ruffian, sir, whose life I have
60 spared at suit of his gray beard —
61 KENT Thou whoreson zed, thou unnecessary letter! My
62 lord, if you will give me leave, I will tread this unbolted
63 villain into mortar and daub the wall of a jakes with
64 him. Spare my gray beard, you wagtail?
CORNWALL
    Peace, sirrah!
    You beastly knave, know you no reverence?
KENT
    Yes, sir, but anger hath a privilege.
CORNWALL
    Why art thou angry?
KENT
    That such a slave as this should wear a sword,
70 Who wears no honesty. Such smiling rogues as these
71 Like rats oft bite the holy cords atwain
72 Which are too intrinse t' unloose; smooth every passion
73 That in the natures of their lords rebel,
    Being oil to fire, snow to the colder moods;
75 Renege, affirm, and turn their halcyon beaks
76 With every gale and vary of their masters,
    Knowing naught, like dogs, but following.
78 A plague upon your epileptic visage!
79 Smile you my speeches, as I were a fool?
80 Goose, if I had you upon Sarum Plain,
81 I'd drive ye cackling home to Camelot.

---

60 *at suit* at the plea   61 *zed* the letter *z* ("unnecessary" because its sound is
also represented by *s,* and because it is not used in Latin)   62 *unbolted* un-
sifted (as flour or plaster)   63 *jakes* toilet   64 *wagtail* a bird that constantly
wags its tail; hence a nervous or effeminate person   71 *holy cords* sacred
bonds   72 *intrinse* intertwined; *smooth* flatter   73 *rebel* i.e., against reason
75 *Renege* deny; *halcyon* kingfisher; their beaks were said to be usable as
weather vanes   76 *gale . . . vary* changing wind   78 *epileptic* grinning   79
Smile you do you smile at; *as* as if   80 *Sarum Plain* Salisbury Plain, near
Winchester (Oswald is a goose because he is laughing, but it is not clear why
Shakespeare associates geese with Salisbury Plain)   81 *Camelot* legendary
capital of King Arthur, thought to have been on the site of Winchester

CORNWALL
  What, art thou mad, old fellow?

knave
1. *male servant*
2. *liar, troublemaker*

GLOUCESTER
  How fell you out? Say that.

KENT
  No contraries hold more antipathy   84
  Than I and such a knave.

CORNWALL
  Why dost thou call him knave? What is his fault?

KENT
  His countenance likes me not.   87

CORNWALL
  No more perchance does mine, nor his, nor hers.

KENT
  Sir, 'tis my occupation to be plain:
  I have seen better faces in my time   90
  Than stands on any shoulder that I see
  Before me at this instant.

CORNWALL   This is some fellow
  Who, having been praised for bluntness, doth affect   93
  A saucy roughness, and constrains the garb   94
  Quite from his nature. He cannot flatter, he;
  An honest mind and plain – he must speak truth.
  An they will take it, so; if not, he's plain.   97
  These kind of knaves I know which in this plainness
  Harbor more craft and more corrupter ends
  Than twenty silly-ducking observants   100
  That stretch their duties nicely.   101

KENT
  Sir, in good faith, in sincere verity,
  Under th' allowance of your great aspect,

---

84 *contraries* opposites 87 *His . . . not* I don't like his face 93 *affect* adopt
94–95 *constrains . . . nature* forces plain speaking away from its proper function (garb = style of speech; his = its) 97 *An* if; *so* well and good; *he's plain*
his excuse is his bluntness 100 *silly . . . observants* bowing attendants 101
nicely excessively

Whose influence, like the wreath of radiant fire
105 On flick'ring Phoebus' front –
CORNWALL   What mean'st by this?
106 KENT   To go out of my dialect, which you discommend
107 so much. I know, sir, I am no flatterer. He that beguiled
you in a plain accent was a plain knave, which, for my
part, I will not be, though I should win your displea-
110 sure to entreat me to't.
CORNWALL   What was th' offense you gave him?
OSWALD
I never gave him any.
113 It pleased the king his master very late
114 To strike at me, upon his misconstruction;
115 When he, compact, and flattering his displeasure,
Tripped me behind; being down, insulted, railed,
117 And put upon him such a deal of man
118 That worthied him, got praises of the king
119 For him attempting who was self-subdued;
120 And, in the fleshment of this dread exploit,
Drew on me here again.
KENT
122 None of these rogues and cowards
But Ajax is their fool.
CORNWALL   Fetch forth the stocks!
You stubborn ancient knave, you reverent braggart,
We'll teach you.
KENT   Sir, I am too old to learn.
Call not your stocks for me, I serve the king –
On whose employment I was sent to you;

speech in metamorphosis

---

105 _Phoebus' front_ the sun god's forehead   106 _go . . . dialect_ depart from my
usual way of speaking   107–8 _He . . . you_ whoever deceived you   110 _to . . ._
_to't_ i.e., even if you begged me to be a knave   113 _very late_ recently   114
misconstruction misunderstanding me   115 _compact_ in league with (the
king)   117 _deal . . . man_ macho act   118 _worthied him_ made him a hero
119 _For . . . subdued_ for attacking a man who refused to fight   120 _flesh-_
ment excitement   122–23 _None . . . fool_ (i.e., Oswald is making a fool out of
Cornwall, whom Kent identifies with the dull-witted and boastful Greek
hero Ajax)

You shall do small respect, show too bold malice
Against the grace and person of my master,
Stocking his messenger.   130

CORNWALL
Fetch forth the stocks. As I have life and honor,
There shall he sit till noon.

REGAN
Till noon? Till night, my lord, and all night too.

KENT
Why, madam, if I were your father's dog,
You should not use me so.

REGAN   Sir, being his knave, I will.   136

CORNWALL
This is a fellow of the selfsame color
Our sister speaks of. Come, bring away the stocks.   138
        Stocks brought out.

GLOUCESTER
Let me beseech your grace not to do so.
[His fault is much, and the good king his master   140
Will check him for't. Your purposed low correction
Is such as basest and contemnèd'st wretches
For pilf'rings and most common trespasses
Are punished with.]   *Cornwall doesn't want*
The king his master needs must take it ill *to let Lear punish*
That he, so slightly valued in his messenger, *his own men.*
Should have him thus restrained.   147

CORNWALL   I'll answer that.

REGAN   *doesn't take*
My sister may receive it much more worse, *Gloucester's*
To have her gentleman abused, assaulted, *advice.*
[For following her affairs. Put in his legs.]   150
        [Kent is put in the stocks.]

CORNWALL
Come, my lord, away!
                Exit [with all but Gloucester and Kent].

---

136 *being* as you are   138 *away* forward   147 *answer* answer for

GLOUCESTER

    I am sorry for thee, friend. 'Tis the duke's pleasure,

    Whose disposition all the world well knows

154   Will not be rubbed nor stopped. I'll entreat for thee.

KENT

155   Pray do not, sir, I have watched and traveled hard.

    Some time I shall sleep out, the rest I'll whistle.

157   A good man's fortune may grow out at heels.

    Give you good morrow.

GLOUCESTER

    The duke's to blame in this. 'Twill be ill taken.   *Exit.*

KENT

160   Good king, that must approve the common saw,

161   Thou out of heaven's benediction com'st

    To the warm sun.

163   Approach, thou beacon to this under globe,

164   That by thy comfortable beams I may

165   Peruse this letter. Nothing almost sees miracles

    But misery. I know 'tis from Cordelia,

    Who hath most fortunately been informed

168   Of my obscurèd course. And shall find time

    From this enormous state, seeking to give

170   Losses their remedies. – All weary and o'erwatched,

171   Take vantage, heavy eyes, not to behold

    This shameful lodging. Fortune, good night;

173   Smile once more; turn thy wheel.

    [Sleeps.]

---

154 *rubbed* deflected (term from the game of bowls) 155 *watched* stayed awake 157 *grow . . . heels* wear thin 160 *approve . . . saw* prove the truth of the old saying 161–62 *Thou . . . sun* you go from God's blessing into the hot sun – i.e., you go from good to bad 163 *beacon* presumably the moon, since it is still night 164 *comfortable* comforting 165–66 *Nothing . . . misery* miracles are rarely seen by any but the miserable 168 *obscurèd* disguised 168–70 *And . . . remedies* (a famously incoherent crux: is Kent reading a bit of Cordelia's letter? [enormous state = terrible situation]) 170 *o'erwatched* too long without sleep 171 *Take vantage* take advantage (by falling asleep) 173 *turn . . . wheel* change my luck: the goddess Fortuna is depicted with a large vertical wheel, which she turns arbitrarily; Kent is now at the bottom

*

∾ **II.3** *Enter Edgar.*

EDGAR
I heard myself proclaimed,   1
And by the happy hollow of a tree   2
Escaped the hunt. No port is free, no place
That guard and most unusual vigilance
Does not attend my taking. Whiles I may scape,   5
I will preserve myself; and am bethought   6
To take the basest and most poorest shape
That ever penury, in contempt of man,   8
Brought near to beast: my face I'll grime with filth,
Blanket my loins, elf all my hairs in knots,   10
And with presented nakedness outface   11
The winds and persecutions of the sky.
The country gives me proof and precedent   13
Of Bedlam beggars, who, with roaring voices,   14
Strike in their numbed and mortified bare arms   15
Pins, wooden pricks, nails, sprigs of rosemary;
And with this horrible object, from low farms,   17
Poor pelting villages, sheepcotes, and mills,   18
Sometimes with lunatic bans, sometime with prayers,   19
Enforce their charity. Poor Turlygod, poor Tom,   20
That's something yet: Edgar I nothing am.   21
                                               Exit.

*

II.3 s.d. Kent remains onstage in the stocks, asleep, but he and Edgar are clearly not part of the same scene. 1 *proclaimed* i.e., as an outlaw 2 *happy hollow* i.e., lucky hiding place 5 *attend . . . taking* prepare to arrest me 6 *am bethought* have a plan 8 *of* for 10 *elf* tangle (into "elf locks") 11 *presented* the show of 13 *proof* experience 14 *Bedlam beggars* (see I.2.136) 15 *Strike* stick; *mortified* dead to pain 17 *object* spectacle 18 *pelting* paltry 19 *bans* curses 20 *Turlygod* (unexplained, but evidently another name for a Bedlam beggar) 21 *Edgar* i.e., as Edgar

❧ **II.4** *Enter Lear, Fool, and Gentleman.*

LEAR
  'Tis strange that they should so depart from home,
  And not send back my messenger.
GENTLEMAN   As I learned,
3 The night before there was no purpose in them
  Of this remove.
KENT   Hail to thee, noble master.
LEAR Ha!
  Mak'st thou this shame thy pastime?
KENT   No, my lord.
7 FOOL Ha, ha, he wears cruel garters. Horses are tied by
  the heads, dogs and bears by th' neck, monkeys by th'
9 loins, and men by th' legs. When a man's overlusty at
10 legs, then he wears wooden netherstocks.
LEAR
  What's he that hath so much thy place mistook
  To set thee here?
KENT   It is both he and she,
13 Your son and daughter.
LEAR No.
KENT Yes.
LEAR No, I say.
KENT I say yea.
[LEAR No, no, they would not.
KENT Yes, they have.]
LEAR
20 By Jupiter, I swear no!
KENT
21 By Juno, I swear ay!

II.4 **3–4** *there . . . remove* they had no intention of leaving **7** *cruel* punning on "crewel," worsted cloth **9** *overlusty . . . legs* too eager to run **10**
netherstocks stockings **13** *son* i.e., son-in-law **21** *Juno* queen of the gods,
wife of Jupiter

LEAR   They durst not do't;
　　They could not, would not do't. 'Tis worse than murder
　　To do upon respect such violent outrage.   23
　　Resolve me with all modest haste which way   24
　　Thou mightst deserve or they impose this usage,
　　Coming from us.
KENT   My lord, when at their home
　　I did commend your highness' letters to them,   27
　　Ere I was risen from the place that showed
　　My duty kneeling, came there a reeking post,   29
　　Stewed in his haste, half breathless, panting forth   30
　　From Goneril his mistress salutations;
　　Delivered letters, spite of intermission,   32
　　Which presently they read; on whose contents   33
　　They summoned up their meiny, straight took horse,   34
　　Commanded me to follow and attend
　　The leisure of their answer, gave me cold looks;
　　And meeting here the other messenger,
　　Whose welcome I perceived had poisoned mine,
　　Being the very fellow which of late
　　Displayed so saucily against your highness,   40
　　Having more man that wit about me, drew;   41
　　He raised the house with loud and coward cries.
　　Your son and daughter found this trespass worth
　　The shame which here it suffers.
FOOL   Winter's not gone yet, if the wild geese fly that   45
　　way.
　　　　　　Fathers that wear rags
　　　　　　　Do make their children blind,   48

---

23 *upon respect* to one who should be respected (as the king's messenger) **24**
Resolve explain to; *modest* decent **27** *commend* deliver **29–30** *reeking . . .*
Stewed hot and sweaty messenger **32** *spite . . . intermission* though he was
interrupting me **33** *presently* immediately **34** *meiny* retinue **40** *Dis-*
played behaved **41** *wit* sense; *drew* drew my sword **45** *Winter's . . . way* if
the geese are flying south ("that way," the way they fly in winter), winter's not
over yet; i.e., things will get worse **48** *blind* (to their father's needs)

49   But fathers that bear bags
50   Shall see their children kind.
        Fortune, that arrant whore,
52   Ne'er turns the key to th' poor.
53 But for all this, thou shalt have as many dolors for thy
54 daughters as thou canst tell in a year.

LEAR
55 O, how this mother swells up toward my heart!
56 *Hysterica passio,* down, thou climbing sorrow;
57 Thy element's below. Where is this daughter?

KENT
    With the earl, sir, here within.

LEAR   Follow me not;
    Stay here.   *Exit.*

GENTLEMAN
60 Made you no more offense but what you speak of?

KENT   None.
    How chance the king comes with so small a number?

63 FOOL   An thou hadst been set i' th' stocks for that ques-
    tion, thou'dst well deserved it.

KENT   Why, fool?

66 FOOL   We'll set thee to school to an ant, to teach thee
    there's no laboring i' th' winter. All that follow their
    noses are led by their eyes but blind men, and there's
    not a nose among twenty but can smell him that's
70 stinking. Let go thy hold when a great wheel runs down
    a hill, lest it break thy neck with following. But the
    great one that goes upward, let him draw thee after.
    When a wise man gives thee better counsel, give me

---

49 *bags* moneybags   52 *turns the key* opens the door   53 *dolors* sorrows,
punning on "dollars," the international European currency   54 *tell* count
55 *mother* hysteria   56 *Hysterica passio* the medical term for hysteria   57
Thy . . . below (hysteria's natural place ["element"] was said to be the ab-
domen or, in women, the womb)   63 *An* if   66–67 *We'll . . . winter* (ants
proverbially do not work in winter – implying that working for Lear is now
unprofitable)

mine again. I would have none but knaves follow it　74
since a fool gives it.
> That sir which serves and seeks for gain,
>> And follows but for form,　　　　　　　77
> Will pack when it begins to rain　　　　78
>> And leave thee in the storm.
> But I will tarry; the fool will stay,　　　80
>> And let the wise man fly.
> The knave turns fool that runs away;　　82
>> The fool no knave, perdy.　　　　83

KENT　Where learned you this, fool?

FOOL　Not i' th' stocks, fool.

Enter Lear and Gloucester.

LEAR
Deny to speak with me? They are sick, they are weary,
They have traveled all the night? Mere fetches,　87
The images of revolt and flying off!　88
Fetch me a better answer.

GLOUCESTER　　　　　　　My dear lord,　90
You know the fiery quality of the duke,
How unremovable and fixed he is
In his own course.

LEAR
Vengeance, plague, death, confusion!
Fiery? What quality? Why, Gloucester, Gloucester,
I'd speak with the Duke of Cornwall and his wife.

GLOUCESTER
Well, my good lord, I have informed them so.

LEAR
Informed them? Dost thou understand me, man?

GLOUCESTER　Ay, my good lord.

LEAR
The king would speak with Cornwall. The dear father

---

74 *again* back　77 *form* show　78 *pack* leave　82 *knave . . . away* i.e., dis-
loyalty is the real folly　83 *perdy* by God (*par Dieu*)　87 *fetches* pretenses
88 *images* signs; *flying off* insurrection　90 *quality* disposition

100   Would with his daughter speak, commands – tends –
      service.
      Are they informed of this? My breath and blood!
      Fiery? The fiery duke, tell the hot duke that –
      No, but not yet. Maybe he is not well.
104   Infirmity doth still neglect all office
105   Whereto our health is bound. We are not ourselves
      When nature, being oppressed, commands the mind
      To suffer with the body. I'll forbear;
108   And am fallen out with my more headier will
109   To take the indisposed and sickly fit
110   For the sound man. – Death on my state! Wherefore
111   Should he sit here? This act persuades me
112   That this remotion of the duke and her
113   Is practice only. Give me my servant forth.
      Go tell the duke and's wife I'd speak with them!
115   Now, presently! Bid them come forth and hear me,
      Or at their chamber door I'll beat the drum
117   Till it cry sleep to death.

GLOUCESTER
      I would have all well betwixt you.   *Exit.*

LEAR
      O me, my heart, my rising heart! But down!
120 FOOL   Cry to it, nuncle, as the cockney did to the eels
121   when she put 'em i' th' paste alive. She knapped 'em o'
122   th' coxcombs with a stick and cried, "Down, wantons,

---

100 *tends – service* awaits their obedience   104 *still . . . office* always neglects duty   105 *Whereto . . . bound* which in health we are bound to obey   108 *fallen out* angry; *headier* headstrong   109 *To take* that mistook   110 *Death . . . state* (the expletive is ironic: "Let my royal power die")   111 *he* Kent   112 *remotion* either removal (from their home) or aloofness (from Lear)   113 *practice* trickery; *Give . . . forth* release my servant   115 *presently* instantly   117 *Till . . . death* till it kills sleep with the noise   120 *cockney* Londoner (i.e., a city dweller)   121 *paste* pastry   121–22 *knapped 'em o' th' coxcombs* knocked them on the head   122 *wantons* rascals, with a quibble on lechers and on deflating erections

down!" 'Twas her brother that, in pure kindness to his
horse, buttered his hay.   124

Enter Cornwall, Regan, Gloucester, Servants.

LEAR
Good morrow to you both.

CORNWALL   Hail to your grace.
Kent here set at liberty.

REGAN
I am glad to see your highness.

LEAR
Regan, I think you are. I know what reason
I have to think so. If thou shouldst not be glad,
I would divorce me from thy mother's tomb,
Sepulch'ring an adult'ress. *[To Kent]* O, are you free?   130
Some other time for that. – Beloved Regan,
Thy sister's naught. O Regan, she hath tied   132
Sharp-toothed unkindness, like a vulture, here.
I can scarce speak to thee. Thou'lt not believe
With how depraved a quality – O Regan!

REGAN
I pray you, sir, take patience. I have hope
You less know how to value her desert   137
Than she to scant her duty.

LEAR   Say? How is that?

REGAN
I cannot think my sister in the least
Would fail her obligation. If, sir, perchance   140
She have restrained the riots of your followers,
'Tis on such ground, and to such wholesome end,
As clears her from all blame.

---

124 *buttered . . . hay* (another example of misguided kindness: horses will
not eat grease)   130 *Sepulch'ring . . . adult'ress* i.e., it would prove you were
not my daughter   132 *naught* wicked (cf. naughty)   137–38 *You . . . duty*
the problem is that you are unable to evaluate her merit rather than that she
has failed in her duty

in the movie,
nature is feminine

LEAR
　My curses on her!
REGAN　　　　　O, sir, you are old;
145　Nature in you stands on the very verge
　Of his confine. You should be ruled, and led　　*estate*
147　By some discretion that discerns your state
　Better than you yourself. Therefore I pray you
　That to our sister you do make return;
150　Say you have wronged her.
LEAR　　　　　　　　　　Ask her forgiveness?
151　Do you but mark how this becomes the house:
　"Dear daughter, I confess that I am old.
　　[Kneels.]
153　Age is unnecessary. On my knees I beg
　That you'll vouchsafe me raiment, bed, and food."
REGAN
　Good sir, no more. These are unsightly tricks.
　Return you to my sister.
LEAR　*[Rises.]*　　　　　Never, Regan.
157　She hath abated me of half my train,
　Looked black upon me, struck me with her tongue
　Most serpentlike upon the very heart.
160　All the stored vengeances of heaven fall
161　On her ingrateful top! Strike her young bones,
162　You taking airs, with lameness.
CORNWALL　　　　　　　　Fie, sir, fie!
LEAR
　You nimble lightnings, dart your blinding flames
　Into her scornful eyes! Infect her beauty,
165　You fen-sucked fogs drawn by the pow'rful sun
　To fall and blister –

145–46 *Nature . . . confine* your life stands at the very edge of its allotted
space　147 *discretion . . . state* discerning person who understands your condition　151 *house* family　153 *Age is* old people are　157 *abated* deprived
161 *top* head　162 *taking airs* infectious vapors　165 *fen-sucked . . . sun* (the
sun was believed to draw infectious vapors from swamps)

REGAN   O the blessed gods!
So will you wish on me when the rash mood is on.
LEAR
No, Regan, thou shalt never have my curse.
Thy tender-hefted nature shall not give   169
Thee o'er to harshness. Her eyes are fierce, but thine   170
Do comfort, and not burn. 'Tis not in thee
To grudge my pleasures, to cut off my train,
To bandy hasty words, to scant my sizes,   173
And, in conclusion, to oppose the bolt   174
Against my coming in. Thou better know'st
The offices of nature, bond of childhood,   176
Effects of courtesy, dues of gratitude.   177
Thy half o' th' kingdom hast thou not forgot,
Wherein I thee endowed.   179
REGAN   Good sir, to th' purpose.
     Tucket within.
LEAR
Who put my man i' th' stocks?   180
CORNWALL   What trumpet's that?
REGAN
I know't – my sister's. This approves her letter   182
That she would soon be here.
     Enter Steward [Oswald].   Is your lady come?
LEAR
This is a slave, whose easy-borrowed pride   184
Dwells in the fickle grace of her he follows.
Out, varlet, from my sight.   186
CORNWALL   What means your grace?
LEAR
Who stocked my servant? Regan, I have good hope

---

169 *tender-hefted* gently disposed   173 *sizes* allowance   174 *oppose the bolt*
bolt the door   176 *offices* duties   177 *Effects* obligations   179 *to . . . pur-*
pose get to the point   182 *approves* confirms   184 *easy-borrowed* impudently
assumed   186 *varlet* scoundrel; *on't* of it

Thou didst not know on't.
    Enter Goneril.   Who comes here? O heavens!
189 If you do love old men, if your sweet sway
190 Allow obedience, if you yourselves are old,
Make it your cause. Send down, and take my part.
    [To Goneril]
Art not ashamed to look upon this beard?
O Regan, will you take her by the hand?

GONERIL
Why not by th' hand, sir? How have I offended?
195 All's not offense that indiscretion finds
196 And dotage terms so.

LEAR   O sides, you are too tough!
Will you yet hold? How came my man i' th' stocks?

CORNWALL
I set him there, sir; but his own disorders
199 Deserved much less advancement.

LEAR   You? Did you?

REGAN
200 I pray you, father, being weak, seem so.
If till the expiration of your month
You will return and sojourn with my sister,
Dismissing half your train, come then to me.
204 I am now from home, and out of that provision
205 Which shall be needful for your entertainment.

LEAR
Return to her, and fifty men dismissed?
No, rather I abjure all roofs, and choose
208 To wage against the enmity o' th' air,
To be a comrade with the wolf and owl,
210 Necessity's sharp pinch. Return with her?
Why, the hot-blooded France, that dowerless took

189–90 *If . . . obedience* if you permit gentle rule to be obeyed **195** *indiscretion* poor judgment **196** *sides* breast (which should burst with grief)
199 *less advancement* less of a promotion – i.e., a worse punishment **204** *from* away from **205** *entertainment* reception **208** *wage* fight

Our youngest born, I could as well be brought
To knee his throne, and, squirelike, pension beg   213
To keep base life afoot. Return with her?
Persuade me rather to be slave and sumpter   215
To this detested groom. *would rather stay with*
GONERIL   At your choice, sir. *Cordelia*
LEAR
I prithee, daughter, do not make me mad.
I will not trouble thee, my child; farewell. *space*
We'll no more meet, no more see one another.
But yet thou art my flesh, my blood, my daughter;   220
Or rather a disease that's in my flesh, *finally dismisses*
Which I must needs call mine. Thou art a boil, *someone for*
A plague-sore, or embossèd carbuncle   *the right* 23
In my corrupted blood. But I'll not chide thee. *reasons,*
Let shame come when it will, I do not call it. *though this*
I do not bid the thunder-bearer shoot, *time he's the 26 one*
Nor tell tales of thee to high-judging Jove. *who's dismisses*
Mend when thou canst, be better at thy leisure;
I can be patient, I can stay with Regan,
I and my hundred knights.   230
                          → space
REGAN
Not altogether so.
I looked not for you yet, nor am provided
For your fit welcome. Give ear, sir, to my sister; *reason*
For those that <u>mingle reason with your passion</u> *vs.*   234
Must be content to think you old and so – *passion*
But she knows what she does.
LEAR   Is this well spoken?
REGAN
I dare avouch it, sir. What, fifty followers?   237
Is it not well? What should you need of more?
Yea, or so many, sith that both charge and danger   239

---

213 *knee* kneel to   215 *sumpter* packhorse   223 *embossèd carbuncle* swollen
tumor   226 *the thunder-bearer* Jove   234 *mingle . . . passion* deal rationally
with your intemperate behavior   237 *avouch* swear   239 *sith that* since;
charge expense

240 Speak 'gainst so great a number? How in one house
Should many people, under two commands,
Hold amity? 'Tis hard, almost impossible.

GONERIL
Why might not you, my lord, receive attendance
From those that she calls servants, or from mine?

REGAN
245 Why not, my lord? If then they chanced to slack ye,
We could control them. If you will come to me
(For now I spy a danger), I entreat you
To bring but five-and-twenty. To no more
249 Will I give place or notice.

LEAR ⤷ *space*
250 I gave you all.

REGAN And in good time you gave it.

LEAR
251 Made you my guardians, my depositaries,
252 But kept a reservation to be followed
With such a number. What, must I come to you
With five-and-twenty? Regan, said you so?

REGAN
And speak't again, my lord. No more with me.

LEAR
256 Those wicked creatures yet do look well-favored
When others are more wicked; not being the worst
258 Stands in some rank of praise.
    [To Goneril] I'll go with thee.
Thy fifty yet doth double five-and-twenty,
260 And thou art twice her love.

GONERIL Hear me, my lord.
What need you five-and-twenty? ten? or five?
To follow in a house where twice so many
Have a command to tend you?

---

245 *slack* neglect 249 *notice* recognition 251 *depositaries* trustees 252 *kept . . . be* stipulated that I be 256 *well-favored* attractive 258 *Stands . . . of* deserves at least some 260 *twice . . . love* twice as loving as she

love isn't measured in space of words or land

REGAN   What need one?
LEAR
  O reason not the need! Our basest beggars *vs.* 264
  Are in the poorest thing superfluous.   *need* 265
  Allow not nature more than nature needs, 266
  Man's life is cheap as beast's. Thou art a lady:
  If only to go warm were gorgeous, 268
  Why, nature needs not what thou gorgeous wear'st,
  Which scarcely keeps thee warm. But, for true need – *270*
  You heavens, give me that patience, patience I need.
  You see me here, you gods, a poor old man,
  As full of grief as age, wretched in both.
  If it be you that stirs these daughters' hearts
  Against their father, fool me not so much 275
  To bear it tamely; touch me with noble anger,
  And let not women's weapons, water drops,
  Stain my man's cheeks. No, you unnatural hags!
  I will have such revenges on you both
  That all the world shall – I will do such things – *280*
  What they are, yet I know not; but they shall be
  The terrors of the earth. You think I'll weep.
  No, I'll not weep.
     Storm and tempest.
  I have full cause of weeping, but this heart
  Shall break into a hundred thousand flaws 285
  Or ere I'll weep. O fool, I shall go mad! 286
     Exeunt [Lear, Fool, Kent, and Gloucester].
CORNWALL
  Let us withdraw; 'twill be a storm.
REGAN
  This house is little; the old man and's people
  Cannot be well bestowed.

------

264 *reason* calculate 265 *Are . . . superfluous* have something more than is
absolutely necessary 266 *Allow not* if you do not grant 268 *If . . . gorgeous*
if warmth were the measure of fashionable dress 275 *fool . . . To* don't make
me such a fool as to 285 *flaws* fragments 286 *Or ere* before

GONERIL

290 'Tis his own blame; hath put himself from rest
And must needs taste his folly.

REGAN

292 For his particular, I'll receive him gladly,
But not one follower.

GONERIL   So am I purposed.
Where is my lord of Gloucester?

CORNWALL
Followed the old man forth.
        [Enter Gloucester.]   He is returned.

GLOUCESTER
The king is in high rage.

CORNWALL   Whither is he going?

GLOUCESTER
He calls to horse, but will I know not whither.

CORNWALL
'Tis best to give him way; he leads himself.

GONERIL
My lord, entreat him by no means to stay.

GLOUCESTER

300 Alack, the night comes on, and the high winds
301 Do sorely ruffle. For many miles about
There's scarce a bush.

REGAN   O, sir, to willful men
The injuries that they themselves procure
Must be their schoolmasters. Shut up your doors.

305 He is attended with a desperate train,
306 And what they may incense him to, being apt
To have his ear abused, wisdom bids fear.

CORNWALL   *Lear = storm*
Shut up your doors, my lord; 'tis a wild night.
My Regan counsels well. Come out o' th' storm.

                                                    Exeunt.

---

292 *his particular* himself alone   301 *ruffle* rage   305 *desperate train* violent
troop   306–7 *apt . . . abused* i.e., likely to be misled

*

∞ **III.1** *Storm still. Enter Kent [disguised] and a*
    Gentleman severally.

KENT
  Who's there besides foul weather?   *again, storm is personified* [handwritten]

GENTLEMAN
  One minded like the weather, most unquietly.

KENT
  I know you. Where's the king?

GENTLEMAN
  Contending with the fretful elements;   4
  Bids the wind blow the earth into the sea,
  Or swell the curlèd waters 'bove the main,   6
  That things might change or cease; [tears his white hair,
  Which the impetuous blasts, with eyeless rage,   8
  Catch in their fury and make nothing of;
  Strives in his little world of man to outscorn   10
  The to-and-fro-conflicting wind and rain. → *Regan & Goneril* [handwritten]
  This night, wherein the cub-drawn bear would couch,   12
  The lion and the belly-pinchèd wolf   13
  Keep their fur dry, unbonneted he runs,
  And bids what will take all.]   15

KENT   But who is with him?

GENTLEMAN
  None but the fool, who labors to outjest   16
  His heart-struck injuries.

KENT   Sir, I do know you,
  And dare upon the warrant of my note   18

III.1 A heath **s.d.** *severally* at different doors   4 *fretful elements* angry weather
6 *main* mainland   8 *eyeless* blind   12 *cub-drawn* sucked dry by her cub, and
therefore ravenous; *couch* stay inside   13 *belly-pinchèd* starving   15 *bids . . .*
will commands whatever wishes to   16 *outjest* overcome with jesting   18
my note what I have observed about you

19 Commend a dear thing to you. There is division,
20 Although as yet the face of it is covered
     With mutual cunning, 'twixt Albany and Cornwall;
22 Who have – as who have not, that their great stars
23 Throned and set high? – servants, who seem no less,
24 Which are to France the spies and speculations
     Intelligent of our state. What hath been seen,
26 Either in snuffs and packings of the dukes,
27 Or the hard rein which both of them have borne
     Against the old kind king, or something deeper,
29 Whereof, perchance, these are but furnishings –
30 [But, true it is, from France there comes a power
     Into this scattered kingdom, who already,
32 Wise in our negligence, have secret feet
33 In some of our best ports and are at point
     To show their open banner. Now to you:
35 If on my credit you dare build so far
     To make your speed to Dover, you shall find
     Some that will thank you, making just report
     Of how unnatural and bemadding sorrow
39 The king hath cause to plain.
40 I am a gentleman of blood and breeding,
     And from some knowledge and assurance offer
42 This office to you.]

GENTLEMAN
     I will talk further with you.

KENT   No, do not.
     For confirmation that I am much more
45 Than my outwall, open this purse and take
     What it contains. If you shall see Cordelia,

---

19 *Commend . . . thing* entrust a precious matter; *division* dissension   **22** *that . . . stars* whom destiny has   **23** *who . . . less* i.e., who really appear to be servants   **24** *speculations . . . Intelligent* observant informers   **26** *snuffs and packings* quarrels and intrigues   **27** *hard rein* harsh treatment; *borne* used   **29** *furnishings* pretexts   **32** *Wise in* knowing of; *secret feet* secretly set foot   **33** *at point* ready   **35** *If . . . build* if you trust me   **39** *plain* complain   **42** *office* undertaking   **45** *outwall* outward appearance

As fear not but you shall, show her this ring,
And she will tell you who that fellow is   48
That yet you do not know. Fie on this storm!
I will go seek the king.   50
GENTLEMAN
Give me your hand. Have you no more to say?
KENT
Few words, but, to effect, more than all yet: 52
That when we have found the king – in which your pain   53
That way, I'll this – he that first lights on him
Holla the other.   *Exeunt [severally].*

*

∾ **III.2** *Storm still. Enter Lear and Fool.*

LEAR
  Blow, winds, and crack your cheeks! Rage, blow!   1
  You cataracts and hurricanoes, spout   2
  Till you have drenched our steeples, drowned the cocks.   3
  You sulph'rous and thought-executing fires,   4
  Vaunt-couriers of oak-cleaving thunderbolts,   5
  Singe my white head. And thou, all-shaking thunder,
  Strike flat the thick rotundity o' th' world,
  Crack nature's molds, all germens spill at once,   8
  That makes ingrateful man.
FOOL O nuncle, court holy water in a dry house is bet-   10
ter than this rainwater out o' door. Good nuncle, in;
ask thy daughters blessing. Here's a night pities neither
wise men nor fools.

---

48 *who . . . is* i.e., who I am 52 *to effect* in importance 53–54 *your . . .
way* in your efforts, go that way
   III.2 Elsewhere on the heath 1 *crack . . . cheeks* (as winds are represented
on old maps, heads with cheeks puffed out) 2 *cataracts . . . hurricanoes* tor-
rential rains and hurricanes 3 *cocks* weather vanes 4 *thought-executing* either annihilating thought or acting as fast as thought 5 *Vaunt-couriers*
heralds 8 *Nature's molds* (in which life is given form); *germens* seeds 10
court holy water flattery

LEAR
    Rumble thy bellyful. Spit, fire. Spout, rain.
    Nor rain, wind, thunder, fire are my daughters.
16   I tax not you, you elements, with unkindness.
    I never gave you kingdom, called you children;
18   You owe me no subscription. Then let fall
    Your horrible pleasure. Here I stand your slave,
20   A poor, infirm, weak, and despised old man.
21   But yet I call you servile ministers,
    That will with two pernicious daughters join
23   Your high-engendered battles 'gainst a head
    So old and white as this. O, ho! 'tis foul.
FOOL   He that has a house to put's head in has a good
26   headpiece.   *space*
27   The codpiece that will house
              Before the head has any,
29   The head and he shall louse:
30   So beggars marry many.
31   The man that makes his toe ·
              What he his heart should make
              Shall of a corn cry woe,
              And turn his sleep to wake.
35   For there was never yet fair woman but she made
    mouths in a glass.
    Enter Kent [disguised].
LEAR
    No, I will be the pattern of all patience;
    I will say nothing.
KENT   Who's there?

---

16 *tax* charge 18 *subscription* deference 21 *ministers* agents 23 *high-engendered battles* heavenly batallions 26 *headpiece* both helmet and brain 27 *codpiece* the pouch for the genitals on men's breeches, here used for the penis; *house* lodge (in copulation) 29–30 *The . . . many* will infest both the head and the codpiece with lice, and end in married poverty 31–32 *The . . . make* (a parallel instance of preferring the lower part to the higher) 35–36 *made . . . glass* practiced smiling in a mirror – i.e., was afflicted with vanity

FOOL   Marry, here's grace and a codpiece; that's a wise   40
man and a fool.

KENT

Alas, sir, are you here? Things that love night
Love not such nights as these. The wrathful skies
Gallow the very wanderers of the dark   44
And make them keep their caves. Since I was man,   45
Such sheets of fire, such bursts of horrid thunder,
Such groans of roaring wind and rain, I never
Remember to have heard. Man's nature cannot carry   48
Th' affliction nor the fear.   *image-heavy object*

LEAR   Let the great gods
That keep this dreadful pudder o'er our heads   50
Find out their enemies now. Tremble, thou wretch,
That hast within thee undivulgèd crimes
Unwhipped of justice. Hide thee, thou bloody hand,   53
Thou perjured, and thou simular of virtue   54
That art incestuous. Caitiff, to pieces shake,   55
That under covert and convenient seeming   56
Has practiced on man's life. Close pent-up guilts,   57
Rive your concealing continents and cry   58
These dreadful summoners grace. I am a man
More sinned against than sinning.   60

KENT   Alack, bareheaded?
Gracious my lord, hard by here is a hovel;   61
Some friendship will it lend you 'gainst the tempest.
Repose you there, while I to this hard house
(More harder than the stones whereof 'tis raised,
Which even but now, demanding after you,   65

---

40 *Marry* a mild exclamation, originally an oath on the name of the Virgin
44 *Gallow* frighten   45 *keep* stay inside   48 *carry* endure   50 *pudder* tu-
mult   53 *of* by   54 *simular of* pretender to   55 *Caitiff* wretch   56 *seeming*
hypocrisy   57 *practiced on* plotted against; *Close* secret   58 *Rive* split open
58–59 *cry . . . grace* beg for mercy from these terrible agents of justice (summoners are officers of church courts)   61 *hard* close   65 *demanding* as I was
asking

Denied me to come in) return, and force
67   Their scanted courtesy.
LEAR
        My wits begin to turn.
        Come on, my boy. How dost, my boy? Art cold?
70   I am cold myself. Where is this straw, my fellow?
        The art of our necessities is strange,
        And can make vile things precious. Come, your hovel.
        Poor fool and knave, I have one part in my heart
        That's sorry yet for thee.
FOOL   *[Sings.]*
75   He that has and a little tiny wit,
                With, heigh-ho, the wind and the rain,
77   Must make content with his fortunes fit
78   Though the rain it raineth every day.
LEAR   True, boy. Come, bring us to this hovel.
                                            Exit [with Kent].
80 FOOL   This is a brave night to cool a courtesan. I'll speak
        a prophecy ere I go:
82   When priests are more in word than matter;
83   When brewers mar their malt with water;
84   When nobles are their tailors' tutors,
85   No heretics burned, but wenches' suitors;
            When every case in law is right,
            No squire in debt nor no poor knight;
            When slanders do not live in tongues,
89   Nor cutpurses come not to throngs;
90   When usurers tell their gold i' th' field,
            And bawds and whores do churches build –

---

67 *scanted* deficient   **75** *and* only, even   **77** *make . . . fit* be content with his
lot   **78** (The song refigures Feste's song at the end of *Twelfth Night*.)   **80**
brave . . . courtesan fine night to cool off the lust of a prostitute   **82** *more . . .*
matter preach better than they practice   **83** *mar* dilute   **84** *are . . . tutors*
teach tailors about fashion (i.e., know what they want)   **85** *No . . . suitors* either the only people who burn are lovers (who burn with passion) or the only
heretics who burn are faithless lovers (who burn with venereal disease)   **89**
cutpurses pickpockets   **90** *tell . . . field* count their money openly (because
they have nothing to hide)

Then shall the realm of Albion   92
Come to great confusion.
Then comes the time, who lives to see't,
That going shall be used with feet.   95
This prophecy Merlin shall make, for I live before his
time.   *Exit.*

*

∾ **III.3** *Enter Gloucester and Edmund.*

GLOUCESTER Alack, alack, Edmund, I like not this unnatural dealing. When I desired their leave that I might
pity him, they took from me the use of mine own   3
house, charged me on pain of perpetual displeasure neither to speak of him, entreat for him, or any way sustain him.
EDMUND Most savage and unnatural.
GLOUCESTER Go to; say you nothing. There is division 8
between the dukes, and a worse matter than that. I
have received a letter this night – 'tis dangerous to be 10
spoken – I have locked the letter in my closet. These   11
injuries the king now bears will be revenged home;   12
there is part of a power already footed; we must incline 13
to the king. I will look him and privily relieve him. Go 14
you and maintain talk with the duke, that my charity
be not of him perceived. If he ask for me, I am ill and 16
gone to bed. If I die for it, as no less is threatened me,
the king my old master must be relieved. There is
strange things toward, Edmund; pray you be careful.   19
                                              Exit.

---

92 *Albion* England 95 *going . . . feet* walking will be done on foot (i.e.,
things will be just as they are now)
    III.3 Gloucester's house 3 *pity* take pity on 8 *Go to* be quiet 11 *closet*
(any private room: study, bedroom) 12 *home* thoroughly 13 *power* army;
footed landed; *incline* to side with 14 *look* search for; *privily* secretly 16 *of*
by 19 *toward* impending

EDMUND
20   This courtesy forbid thee shall the duke
      Instantly know, and of that letter too.
22   This seems a fair deserving, and must draw me
      That which my father loses – no less than all.
      The younger rises when the old doth fall.   *Exit.*

                              *

❧ **III.4** *Enter Lear, Kent [disguised], and Fool.*

KENT
      Here is the place, my lord. Good my lord, enter.
      The tyranny of the open night's too rough
3   For nature to endure.
                 Storm still.
LEAR   Let me alone.
KENT   Good my lord, enter here.
LEAR   Wilt break my heart?
KENT
      I had rather break mine own. Good my lord, enter.
LEAR
      Thou think'st 'tis much that this contentious storm
      Invades us to the skin. So 'tis to thee,
10   But where the greater malady is fixed
      The lesser is scarce felt. Thou'dst shun a bear;
      But if thy flight lay toward the roaring sea,
13   Thou'dst meet the bear i' th' mouth. When the mind's
         free,
14   The body's delicate. The tempest in my mind
      Doth from my senses take all feeling else
      Save what beats there. Filial ingratitude,

---

20 *courtesy . . . thee* kindness you have been forbidden to show   22 *fair deserving* action that would deserve a fair reward
      III.4 Before a hovel on the heath   3 *nature* humanity, human frailty   10 *fixed* lodged   13 *i' th' mouth* head-on   13–14 *When . . . free* only when the mind is untroubled   14 *delicate* sensitive to pain

Is it not as this mouth should tear this hand *unnatural*
For lifting food to't? But I will punish home.
No, I will weep no more. In such a night
To shut me out! Pour on; I will endure.   *20*
In such a night as this! O Regan, Goneril,
Your old kind father, whose frank heart gave all –
O, that way madness lies; let me shun that. ✶ ✶ ✶
No more of that.
KENT   Good my lord, enter here.
LEAR
Prithee go in thyself; seek thine own ease.
This tempest will not give me leave to ponder
On things would hurt me more, but I'll go in.   *27*
    [To the Fool]
In, boy; go first. You houseless poverty –
Nay, get thee in. I'll pray, and then I'll sleep.
                                            Exit [Fool].
Poor naked wretches, wheresoe'er you are,   *30*
That bide the pelting of this pitiless storm,   *31*
How shall your houseless heads and unfed sides,
Your looped and windowed raggedness, defend you   *33*
From seasons such as these? O, I have ta'en   *34*
Too little care of this! Take physic, pomp;   *35*
Expose thyself to feel what wretches feel,
That thou mayst shake the superflux to them   *37*
And show the heavens more just.
EDGAR   *[Within]* Fathom and half, fathom and half!   *39*
Poor Tom!   *40*
    Enter Fool.
FOOL   Come not in here, nuncle; here's a spirit. Help
me, help me!

---

17 *as* as if   27 *would* that would   31 *bide* endure, wait out   33 *looped, windowed* both mean full of holes   34 *seasons* weather   35 *Take . . . pomp*
grandeur, purge yourself   37 *shake . . . superflux* pour out your surplus   39
Fathom . . . half nine feet of water (the call of a sailor taking soundings)

KENT
    Give me thy hand. Who's there?
FOOL   A spirit, a spirit. He says his name's poor Tom.
KENT
    What are thou that dost grumble there i' th' straw?
    Come forth.
        Enter Edgar [as Tom o' Bedlam].
47 EDGAR   Away! the foul fiend follows me. Through the
    sharp hawthorn blow the winds. Hum! go to thy bed
    and warm thee.
50 LEAR   Didst thou give all to thy daughters? And art thou
    come to this?
    EDGAR   Who gives anything to poor Tom? whom the
    foul fiend hath led through fire and through flame,
    through ford and whirlpool, o'er bog and quagmire;
55 that hath laid knives under his pillow and halters in his
56 pew, set ratsbane by his porridge, made him proud of
    heart, to ride on a bay trotting horse over four-inched
58 bridges, to course his own shadow for a traitor. Bless
59 thy five wits, Tom's acold. O, do, de, do, de, do, de.
60 Bless thee from whirlwinds, star-blasting, and taking.
    Do poor Tom some charity, whom the foul fiend vexes.
    There could I have him now – and there – and there
    again – and there –
        Storm still.
    LEAR
    Has his daughters brought him to this pass?
    Couldst thou save nothing? Wouldst thou give 'em all?
FOOL   Nay, he reserved a blanket, else we had been all
    shamed.

───────

47–48 *Through . . . winds* (apparently a fragment of a ballad, quoted again at
l. 99)   55–56 *knives, halters, ratsbane* (all temptations to suicide); *halters . . .
pew* nooses on his balcony   56–58 *made . . . bridges* i.e., made him take mad
risks   58 *course . . . traitor* hunt his own shadow as if it were an enemy   59
five wits the constituent parts of intelligence in Renaissance theories of cog-
nition: common wit, imagination, fantasy, estimation, memory   60 *star-
blasting, taking* malignant stars, infection

LEAR

> Now all the plagues that in the pendulous air   68
> Hang fated o'er men's faults light on thy daughters!   69

KENT   He hath no daughters, sir.   70

LEAR

> Death, traitor! Nothing could have subdued nature
> To such a lowness but his unkind daughters.
> Is it the fashion that discarded fathers
> Should have thus little mercy on their flesh?

Judicious punishment – 'twas this flesh begot
Those pelican daughters.   *pelicans*   76

EDGAR   Pillicock sat on Pillicock Hill. Alow, alow, loo,   77
loo!

FOOL   This cold night will turn us all to fools and madmen.   80

EDGAR   Take heed o' th' foul fiend; obey thy parents; 81
keep thy words' justice; swear not; commit not with   82
man's sworn spouse; set not thy sweet heart on proud   83
array. Tom's acold.

LEAR   What hast thou been?

EDGAR   A servingman, proud in heart and mind; that
curled my hair, wore gloves in my cap; served the lust
of my mistress' heart, and did the act of darkness with 87
her; swore as many oaths as I spake words, and broke
them in the sweet face of heaven. One that slept in the 90
contriving of lust, and waked to do it. Wine loved I
deeply, dice dearly; and in woman out-paramoured the   92

---

68 *pendulous* overhanging   69 *fated* ominously   76 *pelican* cannibalistic:
young pelicans were said to feed on their mother's blood   77 *Pillicock . . .
loo* a fragment of a nursery rhyme; pillicock = both an endearment and baby
talk for penis   81 *Take heed* beware; *obey . . . parents* this and the following
injunctions are from the Ten Commandments   82 *keep . . . justice* i.e., do
not lie; *commit not* i.e., do not commit adultery   83–84 *proud array* luxurious clothing   87 *wore . . . cap* as courtly lovers did with tokens from their
mistresses   90–91 *slept . . . lust* went to sleep planning acts of lechery
92–93 *out-paramoured . . . Turk* had more lovers than the Sultan has in his
harem

93   Turk. False of heart, light of ear, bloody of hand; hog in
sloth, fox in stealth, wolf in greediness, dog in madness,
95   lion in prey. Let not the creaking of shoes nor the
rustling of silks betray thy poor heart to woman. Keep
97   thy foot out of brothels, thy hand out of plackets, thy
98   pen from lenders' books, and defy the foul fiend. Still
through the hawthorn blows the cold wind; says suum,
100   mun, nonny. Dolphin my boy, boy, sessa! let him
trot by.
> *Storm still.*

102 LEAR Thou wert better in a grave than to answer with
thy uncovered body this extremity of the skies. Is man
no more than this? Consider him well. Thou ow'st the
worm no silk, the beast no hide, the sheep no wool, the
106 cat no perfume. Ha! here's three on's are sophisticated.
107 Thou art the thing itself; unaccommodated man is no
more but such a poor, bare, forked animal as thou art.
109 Off, off, you lendings! Come, unbutton here.
> *[Begins to disrobe.]*

110 FOOL Prithee, nuncle, be contented; 'tis a naughty night
to swim in. Now a little fire in a wild field were like an
old lecher's heart – a small spark, all the rest on's body
cold. Look, here comes a walking fire.
> *Enter Gloucester with a torch.*

114 EDGAR This is the foul Flibbertigibbet. He begins at
115 curfew, and walks till the first cock. He gives the web
116 and the pin, squints the eye, and makes the harelip;

---

93 *light of ear* attentive to gossip and slander 95–96 *creaking . . . silks* both
fashionable in women 97 *plackets* slits in women's skirts; hence vaginas
98 *pen . . . books* i.e., stay out of debt 100 *Dolphin . . . sessa* unexplained;
possibly a bit of a ballad, possibly a hunting call: Dolphin is usually taken to
refer to the French crown prince, the dauphin, but it sounds more like a
hunting dog's name; sessa (*cessez*) = stop 102 *answer* experience 106 *cat*
civet cat, from whose secretions perfume was made; *on's* of us; *sophisticated*
artificial 107 *unaccommodated* unadorned, unfurnished 109 *lendings* bor-
rowed articles (because not part of his body) 110 *naughty* evil 114 *Flibbertigibbet* in Elizabethan folklore, a dancing devil 115 *curfew* 9 P.M.; *first
cock* midnight 115–16 *the . . . pin* eye cataracts 116 *squints* makes squint

mildews the white wheat, and hurts the poor creature   117
of earth.

> Swithold footed thrice the 'old;   119
> He met the nightmare, and her ninefold;   120
>   Bid her alight   121
>   And her troth plight,   122
> And aroint thee, witch, aroint thee!   123

KENT   How fares your grace?

LEAR   What's he?

KENT   Who's there? What is't you seek?

GLOUCESTER   What are you there? Your names?

EDGAR   Poor Tom, that eats the swimming frog, the
toad, the tadpole, the wall newt and the water; that in   129
the fury of his heart, when the foul fiend rages, eats cow   *130*
dung for sallets, swallows the old rat and the ditch dog,   131
drinks the green mantle of the standing pool; who is   132
whipped from tithing to tithing, and stock-punished   133
and imprisoned; who hath had three suits to his back,
six shirts to his body,

> Horse to ride, and weapon to wear,
> But mice and rats, and such small deer,   137
> Have been Tom's food for seven long year.

Beware my follower! Peace, Smulkin, peace, thou fiend!   139

---

117 *white* almost ripe   119 *Swithold* Saint Withold, invoked as a general protector against harm; *footed . . . 'old* walked the plain (wold) three times   120 *nightmare* incubus, female demon; *ninefold* nine offspring   121 *Bid . . . alight* ordered her to get off (the sleeper's chest)   122 *her troth plight* give her promise (not to do it again)   123 *aroint thee* be gone   129 *wall newt* lizard; *water* i.e., water newt   131 *sallets* delicacies; *ditch dog* dead dog thrown in a ditch   132 *green mantle* scum; *standing* stagnant   133 *tithing* parish; *stock-punished* put in the stocks   137 *deer* game; the jingle is adapted from the popular romance *Bevis of Hampton*   139 *Smulkin* like Modo and Mahu below, devils identified in Samuel Harsnett's *Declaration of Egregious Popish Impostures* (1603)

GLOUCESTER

140   What, hath your grace no better company?

EDGAR

    The prince of darkness is a gentleman.
    Modo he's called, and Mahu.

GLOUCESTER

    Our flesh and blood, my lord, is grown so vile

144   That it doth hate what gets it.

EDGAR   Poor Tom's acold.

GLOUCESTER

146   Go in with me. My duty cannot suffer
    T' obey in all your daughters' hard commands.
    Though their injunction be to bar my doors
    And let this tyrannous night take hold upon you,

150   Yet have I ventured to come seek you out
    And bring you where both fire and food is ready.

LEAR

    First let me talk with this philosopher.
    What is the cause of thunder? *are there gods watching over me?*

KENT

    Good my lord, take his offer; go into th' house. *or are they angry*

LEAR

155   I'll talk a word with this same learnèd Theban. *at me?*

156   What is your study? *if so, why?*

EDGAR

157   How to prevent the fiend, and to kill vermin.

LEAR

    Let me ask you one word in private.

KENT

    Importune him once more to go, my lord.

160   His wits begin t' unsettle.

---

144 *gets* begets   146 *suffer* allow me   155 *learnèd Theban* Greek scholar
156 *study* field of study   157 *prevent* thwart

GLOUCESTER
　Canst thou blame him?
　　Storm still.
　His daughters seek his death. Ah, that good Kent,
　He said it would be thus, poor banished man!
　Thou sayest the king grows mad – I'll tell thee, friend,
　I am almost mad myself. I had a son,
　Now outlawed from my blood; he sought my life   166
　But lately, very late. I loved him, friend,   167
　No father his son dearer. True to tell thee,
　The grief hath crazed my wits. What a night's this!
　I do beseech your grace –   *170*
LEAR
　O, cry you mercy, sir.   171
　Noble philosopher, your company.
EDGAR　Tom's acold.
GLOUCESTER
　In, fellow, there, into th' hovel; keep thee warm.
LEAR　Come, let's in all.
KENT　This way, my lord.
LEAR
　With him!
　I will keep still with my philosopher.
KENT
　Good my lord, soothe him; let him take the fellow.   179
GLOUCESTER　Take him you on.   180
KENT　Sirrah, come on; go along with us.
LEAR　Come, good Athenian.   182
GLOUCESTER　No words, no words! Hush.

---

166 *outlawed . . . blood* disowned, disinherited **167** *late* recently **171**
cry . . . mercy I beg your pardon **179** *soothe* humor **180** *you on* along with
you **182** *Athenian* philosopher

184 EDGAR   Child Rowland to the dark tower came;
185   His word was still "Fie, foh, and fum,
             I smell the blood of a British man."   *Exeunt.*

                        *

∾ **III.5** *Enter Cornwall and Edmund.*

CORNWALL   I will have my revenge ere I depart his house.

3 EDMUND   How, my lord, I may be censured, that nature
4 thus gives way to loyalty, something fears me to think of.

CORNWALL   I now perceive it was not altogether your
7 brother's evil disposition made him seek his death; but
8 a provoking merit, set awork by a reprovable badness in
9 himself.

10 EDMUND   How malicious is my fortune that I must re-
pent to be just! This is the letter which he spoke of,
12 which approves him an intelligent party to the advantages of France. O heavens, that this treason were not
or not I the detector!

CORNWALL   Go with me to the duchess.

EDMUND   If the matter of this paper be certain, you have
mighty business in hand.

CORNWALL   True or false, it hath made thee Earl of
Gloucester. Seek out where thy father is, that he may be
20 ready for our apprehension.

---

184 *Child . . . came* presumably a line from a ballad about the hero of the
Chanson de Roland; child = a knight in training   185–86 *His . . . man* Edgar
switches to a ballad about Jack the Giant Killer; word = motto, still = always
   III.5 Gloucester's house   3 *censured* criticized   3–4 *nature . . . loyalty* (the
contrast is between familial and political bonds)   4 *something . . . me* I am
almost afraid   7 *his* Gloucester's   8 *a . . . awork* a virtue incited to work
9 *himself* Gloucester (i.e., however wicked parricide is, Gloucester got what
he deserved)   12 *approves* proves; *intelligent . . . of* spy on behalf of   20 *apprehension* arrest

EDMUND   *[Aside]* If I find him comforting the king, it   21
will stuff his suspicion more fully. – I will persever in
my course of loyalty, though the conflict be sore between that and my blood.   24
CORNWALL   I will lay trust upon thee, and thou shalt
find a dearer father in my love.   *Exeunt.*

                        *

∾ **III.6** *Enter Kent [disguised] and Gloucester.*

GLOUCESTER   Here is better than the open air; take it
thankfully. I will piece out the comfort with what addi-   2
tion I can. I will not be long from you.
KENT   All the power of his wits have given way to his
impatience. The gods reward your kindness.   5
                        Exit [Gloucester].
     Enter Lear, Edgar, and Fool.
EDGAR   Frateretto calls me, and tells me Nero is an an-   6
gler in the lake of darkness. Pray, innocent, and beware
the foul fiend.
FOOL   Prithee, nuncle, tell me whether a madman be a
gentleman or a yeoman.   10
LEAR
     A king, a king.
FOOL   No, he's a yeoman that has a gentleman to his son;   12
for he's a mad yeoman that sees his son a gentleman
before him.   14
LEAR
To have a thousand with red burning spits
Come hissing in upon 'em –

---

21 *comforting* abetting   24 *blood* family ties
    III.6 Within the hovel   2 *piece out* augment   5 *impatience* passion, rage
6 *Frateretto* another devil from Harsnett's *Declaration* (see III.4.139); *Nero*
the diabolical Roman emperor, here condemned, following Chaucer's Monk's
Tale, to fish in the lake of hell   10 *yeoman* a landowner, but not a gentleman
12 *to* as   14 *before him* i.e., before he himself has been raised to the gentry

[EDGAR   The foul fiend bites my back.

FOOL   He's mad that trusts in the tameness of a wolf, a
horse's health, a boy's love, or a whore's oath.

LEAR

20   It shall be done; I will arraign them straight.
         [To Edgar]
     Come, sit thou here, most learnèd justice.
         [To the Fool]
     Thou, sapient sir, sit here. Now, you she-foxes –

23   EDGAR   Look, where he stands and glares. Want'st thou
     eyes at trial, madam?

25   Come o'er the burn, Bessy, to me.

26   FOOL   Her boat hath a leak,
                       And she must not speak
                     Why she dares not come over to thee.

     EDGAR   The foul fiend haunts poor Tom in the voice of a
30   nightingale. Hoppedance cries in Tom's belly for two
31   white herring. Croak not, black angel; I have no food
     for thee.

KENT

33   How do you, sir? Stand you not so amazed.
     Will you lie down and rest upon the cushions?

LEAR

     I'll see their trial first. Bring in their evidence.
         [To Edgar]
     Thou, robèd man of justice, take thy place.
         [To the Fool]
37   And thou, his yokefellow of equity,

---

20 *arraign . . . straight* put them on trial immediately   23–24 *Want'st . . .
eyes* do you lack for spectators (?); are you blind (?)   25 *Come . . . me* from a
popular ballad; burn = stream (The fool's continuation is an obscene parody,
punning on "burn" as the pain of venereal disease.)   26 *boat . . . leak* both
from the effects of the disease and because women are proverbially "leaky
vessels"   30 *Hoppedance* another devil from Harsnett   31 *white* fresh; *Croak
not* i.e., stop rumbling, belly   33 *amazed* bewildered   37 *yokefellow . . .
equity* fellow judge

Bench by his side. *[To Kent]* You are o' th' commission; 38
Sit you too.

EDGAR   Let us deal justly. 40
          Sleepest or wakest thou, jolly shepherd?
              Thy sheep be in the corn; 42
                  And for one blast of thy minikin mouth 43
              Thy sheep shall take no harm.

Purr, the cat is gray. 45

LEAR   Arraign her first. 'Tis Goneril, I here take my oath
before this honorable assembly, kicked the poor king
her father.

FOOL   Come hither, mistress. Is your name Goneril?

LEAR   She cannot deny it. 50

FOOL   Cry you mercy, I took you for a joint stool. 51

LEAR

And here's another, whose warped looks proclaim
What store her heart is made on. Stop her there! 53
Arms, arms, sword, fire! Corruption in the place! 54
False justicer, why hast thou let her scape?]

EDGAR   Bless thy five wits!

KENT

O pity! Sir, where is the patience now
That you so oft have boasted to retain?

EDGAR   *[Aside]*

My tears begin to take his part so much
They mar my counterfeiting. 60

LEAR

The little dogs and all, 61
Tray, Blanch, and Sweetheart – see, they bark at me.

---

38 *Bench* preside; *o' th' commission* i.e., presiding as a judge   42 *corn* wheat
43 *minikin* pretty little   45 *Purr, the cat* another Harsnett devil, here taking
the form of a cat   51 *I . . . joint stool* I beg your pardon, I mistook you for a
stool – i.e., I didn't notice you; but the stool here is standing in for Goneril
53 *store* material; *on* of   54 *Corruption . . . place* i.e., there's bribery in the
court   61 *The . . . all* even the lapdogs

63 EDGAR   Tom will throw his head at them. Avaunt, you
curs.

65   Be thy mouth or black or white,
        Tooth that poisons if it bite;
        Mastiff, greyhound, mongrel grim,
68   Hound or spaniel, brach or lym,
69   Or bobtail tike, or trundle-tail –
70   Tom will make him weep and wail;
        For, with throwing thus my head,
72   Dogs leaped the hatch, and all are fled.
73 Do, de, de, de. Sessa! Come, march to wakes and fairs
74 and market towns. Poor Tom, thy horn is dry.

75 LEAR   Then let them anatomize Regan. See what breeds
about her heart. Is there any cause in nature that makes
77 these hard hearts? *[To Edgar]* You, sir, I entertain for
one of my hundred; only I do not like the fashion of
79 your garments. You will say they are Persian; but let
80 them be changed.

KENT
Now, good my lord, lie here and rest awhile.

LEAR
82 Make no noise, make no noise; draw the curtains.
So, so. We'll go to supper i' th' morning.

FOOL   And I'll go to bed at noon.
    Enter Gloucester.

GLOUCESTER
Come hither, friend. Where is the king my master?

KENT
Here, sir, but trouble him not; his wits are gone.

---

63 *throw* shake; *Avaunt* get away   65 *or* either   68 *brach . . . lym* bitch or
bloodhound   69 *bobtail . . . trundle-tail* short- or long-tailed mongrel   72
hatch lower half of a Dutch door   73 *Sessa!* stop! (French *cessez*); *wakes* festivals   74 *horn is dry* drinking horn is empty (i.e., "I've run out of steam")
75 *anatomize* dissect   77 **s.d.** (or perhaps addressed to Kent, who has, ironically, been in Lear's service); *entertain* employ   79 *Persian* luxurious   82
curtains i.e., about an imaginary four-poster bed

GLOUCESTER
    Good friend, I prithee take him in thy arms.
    I have o'erheard a plot of death upon him.   88
    There is a litter ready; lay him in't
    And drive toward Dover, friend, where thou shalt meet   90
    Both welcome and protection. Take up thy master.
    If thou shouldst dally half an hour, his life,
    With thine and all that offer to defend him,
    Stand in assurèd loss. Take up, take up,   94
    And follow me, that will to some provision   95
    Give thee quick conduct.
[KENT   .   Oppressèd nature sleeps.
    This rest might yet have balmed thy broken sinews,
    Which, if convenience will not allow,   98
    Stand in hard cure.   99
        [To the Fool]   Come, help to bear thy master.
    Thou must not stay behind.]   *100*
GLOUCESTER   Come, come, away!
                   Exeunt [all but Edgar].

[EDGAR
    When we our betters see bearing our woes,   101
    We scarcely think our miseries our foes.
    Who alone suffers suffers most i' th' mind,
    Leaving free things and happy shows behind;   104
    But then the mind much sufferance doth o'erskip
    When grief hath mates, and bearing fellowship.   106
    How light and portable my pain seems now,   107
    When that which makes me bend makes the king bow.
    He childed as I fatherèd. Tom, away.   109
    Mark the high noises, and thyself bewray   110

---

88 *upon* against   **94** *Stand . . . loss* will surely be lost   **95–96** *to . . . conduct* will quickly lead you to provisions for the journey   **98** *convenience* circumstances   **99** *Stand . . . cure* will be hard to cure   **101** *bearing . . . woes* enduring the same suffering as we do   **104** *free* carefree; *shows* scenes   **106** *bearing fellowship* endurance has company   **107** *portable* bearable   **109** *He* he is   **110** *Mark . . . noises* follow the news of those in power; *bewray* reveal

111 When false opinion, whose wrong thoughts defile thee,
     In thy just proof repeals and reconciles thee.
113 What will hap more tonight, safe scape the king!
     Lurk, lurk.]   *[Exit.]*

                           *

∾ **III.7** *Enter Cornwall, Regan, Goneril, Bastard*
      [Edmund], and Servants.

1 CORNWALL *[To Goneril]* Post speedily to my lord your
     husband; show him this letter. The army of France is
     landed. *[To Servants]* Seek out the traitor Gloucester.
                            [Exeunt some Servants.]
   REGAN Hang him instantly.
   GONERIL Pluck out his eyes.
   CORNWALL Leave him to my displeasure. Edmund, keep
7   you our sister company. The revenges we are bound to
     take upon your traitorous father are not fit for your be-
9   holding. Advise the duke where you are going, to a
10   most festinate preparation. We are bound to the like.
11   Our posts shall be swift and intelligent betwixt us.
12   Farewell, dear sister; farewell, my lord of Gloucester.
         Enter Steward [Oswald].
     How now? Where's the king?
   OSWALD
     My lord of Gloucester hath conveyed him hence.
     Some five or six and thirty of his knights,
16   Hot questrists after him, met him at gate;
     Who, with some other of the lord's dependents,
     Are gone with him toward Dover, where they boast
     To have well-armèd friends.

111–12 *When . . . repeals* when proof of your innocence vindicates 113
What . . . more whatever more happens
   III.7 Gloucester's house 1 *Post* ride 7 *sister* i.e., Goneril 9–10 *a . . .
preparation* prepare quickly 10 *are . . . to* must do 11 *posts* messengers; *intelligent* informative 12 *my . . . Gloucester* (Edmund has been given his father's title) 16 *questrists* searchers

CORNWALL   Get horses for your mistress. *Exit [Oswald].*   20
GONERIL
  Farewell, sweet lord, and sister.
CORNWALL
  Edmund, farewell.

                    [Exeunt Goneril and Edmund.]
               Go seek the traitor Gloucester,
  Pinion him like a thief, bring him before us.   23
                  [Exeunt other Servants.]
  Though well we may not pass upon his life   24
  Without the form of justice, yet our power
  Shall do a court'sy to our wrath, which men   26
  May blame, but not control.
    Enter Gloucester and Servants.
                    Who's there, the traitor?
REGAN
  Ingrateful fox, 'tis he.
CORNWALL
  Bind fast his corky arms.   29
GLOUCESTER
  What means your graces? Good my friends, consider   30
  You are my guests. Do me no foul play, friends.
CORNWALL
  Bind him, I say.
    [Servants bind him.]
REGAN   Hard, hard! O filthy traitor.
GLOUCESTER
  Unmerciful lady as you are, I'm none.
CORNWALL
  To this chair bind him. Villain, thou shalt find –
    [Regan plucks Gloucester's beard.]
GLOUCESTER
  By the kind gods, 'tis most ignobly done
  To pluck me by the beard.   36

---

23 *Pinion him* tie him up   **24** *pass* pass sentence   **26** *do . . . to* defer to   **29**
corky dry, withered   **36** *To . . . beard* (considered an extreme insult)

REGAN
37   So white, and such a traitor?
GLOUCESTER   Naughty lady,
  These hairs which thou dost ravish from my chin
39   Will quicken and accuse thee. I am your host.
40   With robber's hands my hospitable favors
41   You should not ruffle thus. What will you do?
CORNWALL
42   Come, sir, what letters had you late from France?
REGAN
43   Be simple-answered, for we know the truth.
CORNWALL
  And what confederacy have you with the traitors
45   Late footed in the kingdom?
REGAN
  To whose hands you have sent the lunatic king.
  Speak.
GLOUCESTER
48   I have a letter guessingly set down,
  Which came from one that's of a neutral heart,
50   And not from one opposed.
CORNWALL   Cunning.
REGAN   And false.
CORNWALL
  Where hast thou sent the king?
GLOUCESTER
  To Dover.
REGAN
53   Wherefore to Dover? Wast thou not charged at peril –
CORNWALL
  Wherefore to Dover? Let him answer that.

---

37 *Naughty* evil   39 *quicken* come to life   40 *hospitable favors* welcoming face   41 *ruffle* tear at   42 *late* lately   43 *Be simple-answered* answer plainly   45 *Late footed* lately landed   48 *guessingly* speculatively   53 *charged at peril* ordered at peril of your life

GLOUCESTER
  I am tied to th' stake, and I must stand the course.   55
REGAN
  Wherefore to Dover?
GLOUCESTER
  Because I would not see thy cruel nails
  Pluck out his poor old eyes; nor thy fierce sister
  In his anointed flesh stick boarish fangs.   59
  The sea, with such a storm as his bare head   60
  In hell-black night endured, would have buoyed up   61
  And quenched the stellèd fires.   62
  Yet, poor old heart, he holp the heavens to rain.   63
  If wolves had at thy gate howled that stern time,
  Thou shouldst have said, "Good porter, turn the key."   65
  All cruels else subscribe. But I shall see   66
  The wingèd vengeance overtake such children.   67
CORNWALL
  See't shalt thou never. Fellows, hold the chair.
  Upon these eyes of thine I'll set my foot.
GLOUCESTER
  He that will think to live till he be old,   70
  Give me some help. – O cruel! O you gods!
    [Cornwall puts out Gloucester's eye.]
REGAN
  One side will mock another. Th' other too.
CORNWALL
  If you see vengeance –
FIRST SERVANT   Hold your hand, my lord!
  I have served you ever since I was a child;
  But better service have I never done you
  Than now to bid you hold.

---

55 *I . . . course* (the image is from bearbaiting, in which the animal is tied to a stake and attacked by dogs)   59 *anointed* consecrated   61 *buoyed* swelled   62 *stellèd* stellar   63 *holp* helped   65 *turn the key* open the door   66 *All . . . subscribe* all other cruel creatures submit (to feelings of compassion) (?)   67 *wingèd vengeance* avenging Furies

REGAN   How now, you dog?
FIRST SERVANT
  If you did wear a beard upon your chin,
78 I'd shake it on this quarrel. What do you mean!
CORNWALL
79 My villain!
    [Draw and fight.]
FIRST SERVANT
80 Nay, then, come on, and take the chance of anger.
REGAN
  Give me thy sword. A peasant stand up thus?
    [She takes a sword and runs at him behind;] kills him.
FIRST SERVANT
  O, I am slain! My lord, you have one eye left
  To see some mischief on him. O!
CORNWALL
  Lest it see more, prevent it. Out, vile jelly.
    [Puts out Gloucester's other eye.]
  Where is thy luster now?
GLOUCESTER
  All dark and comfortless. Where's my son Edmund?
  Edmund, enkindle all the sparks of nature
88 To quit this horrid act.
REGAN   Out, treacherous villain;
  Thou call'st on him that hates thee. It was he
90 That made the overture of thy treasons to us;
  Who is too good to pity thee.
GLOUCESTER
92 O my follies! Then Edgar was abused.
  Kind gods, forgive me that, and prosper him.

---

78 *shake . . . quarrel* pluck it in this cause; *What . . . mean!* i.e., how dare
you! 79 *villain* (the word retained some of its original meaning of serf or
servant) 80 *chance . . . anger* risk of an angry fight 88 *quit* avenge 90
made . . . of revealed 92 *abused* wronged

REGAN
  Go thrust him out at gates, and let him smell
  His way to Dover.   *Exit [one] with Gloucester.*   95
                    How is't, my lord? How look you?
CORNWALL
  I have received a hurt. Follow me, lady.
  Turn out that eyeless villain. Throw this slave
  Upon the dunghill. Regan, I bleed apace.
  Untimely comes this hurt. Give me your arm.   *Exeunt.*
[SECOND SERVANT
  I'll never care what wickedness I do,   *100*
  If this man come to good.
THIRD SERVANT   If she live long,
  And in the end meet the old course of death,   102
  Women will all turn monsters.
SECOND SERVANT
  Let's follow the old earl, and get the Bedlam
  To lead him where he would. His roguish madness
  Allows itself to anything.   *[Exit.]*
THIRD SERVANT
  Go thou. I'll fetch some flax and whites of eggs
  To apply to his bleeding face. Now heaven, help him.
                                          Exit.]

                         *

⌒ **IV.1** *Enter Edgar.*

EDGAR
  Yet better thus, and known to be contemned,   1
  Than still contemned and flattered. To be worst,   2
  The lowest and most dejected thing of fortune,
  Stands still in esperance, lives not in fear.   4

_____
95 *How . . . you?* how do you feel?   102 *meet . . . death* i.e., die a natural
death
    IV.1 Open country   1 *contemned* despised   2 *still* always   4 *Stands . . .*
esperance always has hope (because he has no fear of falling lower)

The lamentable change is from the best;
6   The worst returns to laughter. Welcome then,
Thou unsubstantial air that I embrace:
The wretch that thou hast blown unto the worst
9   Owes nothing to thy blasts.
       Enter Gloucester and an Old Man.
                                        But who comes here?
10   My father, poorly led? World, world, O world!
11   But that thy strange mutations make us hate thee,
12   Life would not yield to age.
OLD MAN   O my good lord,
       I have been your tenant, and your father's tenant,
       These fourscore years.
GLOUCESTER
       Away, get thee away. Good friend, be gone.
       Thy comforts can do me no good at all;
       Thee they may hurt.
OLD MAN   You cannot see your way.
GLOUCESTER
       I have no way, and therefore want no eyes;
       I stumbled when I saw. Full oft 'tis seen
20   Our means secure us, and our mere defects
21   Prove our commodities. O dear son Edgar,
22   The food of thy abusèd father's wrath,
       Might I but live to see thee in my touch
       I'd say I had eyes again.
OLD MAN   How now? Who's there?
EDGAR   *[Aside]*
       O gods! Who is't can say "I am at the worst"?
       I am worse than e'er I was.
OLD MAN   'Tis poor mad Tom.

---

6 *returns to laughter* i.e., can only get better   **9** *Owes nothing to* is not in-
debted to   **11** *But* except   **12** *yield to age* be reconciled to growing old   **20**
Our . . . us our prosperity makes us overconfident; *mere defects* utter depriva-
tion   **21** *commodities* advantages   **22** *food* prey

EDGAR *[Aside]*
  And worse I may be yet. The worst is not
  So long as we can say "This is the worst."
OLD MAN   Fellow, where goest?
GLOUCESTER   Is it a beggarman?   30
OLD MAN   Madman and beggar too.
GLOUCESTER
  He has some reason, else he could not beg.   32
  I' th' last night's storm I such a fellow saw,
  Which made me think a man a worm. My son
  Came then into my mind, and yet my mind
  Was then scarce friends with him. I have heard more
    since.
  As flies to wanton boys are we to th' gods;   ] - worldly   37
  They kill us for their sport.
EDGAR *[Aside]*   How should this be?
  Bad is the trade that must play fool to sorrow,   39
  Ang'ring itself and others. – Bless thee, master.   40
GLOUCESTER
  Is that the naked fellow?
OLD MAN   Ay, my lord.
GLOUCESTER
  Then prithee get thee gone. If for my sake
  Thou wilt o'ertake us hence a mile or twain
  I' th' way toward Dover, do it for ancient love;   44
  And bring some covering for this naked soul,
  Which I'll entreat to lead me.
OLD MAN   Alack, sir, he is mad.
GLOUCESTER
  'Tis the time's plague when madmen lead the blind.   48

---

32 *reason* sanity **37** *wanton* playful, irresponsible **39** *Bad . . . sorrow* playing the fool in the presence of grief is a bad business **44** *ancient love* our long relationship (as lord and tenant) **48** *time's plague* sickness of the times

Do as I bid thee, or rather do thy pleasure.
50   Above the rest, be gone.

OLD MAN
51   I'll bring him the best 'parel that I have,
52   Come on't what will.   *Exit.*

GLOUCESTER
Sirrah naked fellow –

EDGAR
54   Poor Tom 's acold. *[Aside]* I cannot daub it further.

GLOUCESTER
Come hither, fellow.

EDGAR   *[Aside]*
And yet I must. – Bless thy sweet eyes, they bleed.

GLOUCESTER
Know'st thou the way to Dover?

EDGAR   Both stile and gate, horseway and footpath. Poor
Tom hath been scared out of his good wits. Bless thee,
60   good man's son, from the foul fiend. [Five fiends have
been in poor Tom at once: of lust, as Obidicut; Hobbi-
didence, prince of dumbness; Mahu, of stealing; Modo,
63   of murder; Flibbertigibbet, of mopping and mowing,
who since possesses chambermaids and waiting women.
So, bless thee, master.]

GLOUCESTER
Here, take this purse, thou whom the heavens' plagues
67   Have humbled to all strokes. That I am wretched
Makes thee the happier. Heavens, deal so still!
69   Let the superfluous and lust-dieted man,
70   That slaves your ordinance, that will not see
Because he does not feel, feel your pow'r quickly;
So distribution should undo excess,
And each man have enough. Dost thou know Dover?

---

50 *Above . . . rest* above all   51 *'parel* apparel   52 *Come . . . will* whatever
may come of it   54 *daub it* lay it on – i.e., act the part   63 *mopping . . .
mowing* making faces   67 *humbled to* reduced to bearing meekly   69 *superfluous . . . man* man who has too much and feeds his desires   70 *slaves . . .
ordinance* makes a slave of heaven's injunction (to give to the poor)

EDGAR Ay, master.
GLOUCESTER
  There is a cliff, whose high and bending head   75
  Looks fearfully in the confinèd deep.   76
  Bring me but to the very brim of it,
  And I'll repair the misery thou dost bear
  With something rich about me. From that place
  I shall no leading need.   Give me thy arm.   80
EDGAR
  Poor Tom shall lead thee.   *Exeunt.*

         *   *does Edgar recognize his father?*

∾ **IV.2** *Enter Goneril, Bastard [Edmund], and Steward*
    [Oswald].

GONERIL
  Welcome, my lord. I marvel our mild husband
  Not met us on the way.   2
    [To Oswald]   Now, where's your master?
OSWALD
  Madam, within, but never man so changed.
  I told him of the army that was landed:
  He smiled at it. I told him you were coming:
  His answer was, "The worse." Of Gloucester's treachery
  And of the loyal service of his son
  When I informed him, then he called me sot   8
  And told me I had turned the wrong side out.
  What most he should dislike seems pleasant to him;   10
  What like, offensive.
GONERIL   *[To Edmund]* Then shall you go no further.
  It is the cowish terror of his spirit,   12
  That dares not undertake. He'll not feel wrongs   13

---

75 *bending* overhanging 76 *in . . . deep* over the straits (of the English Channel) below
    IV.2 Before Albany's castle 2 *Not* has not 8 *sot* fool 12 *cowish* cowardly 13 *undertake* commit himself to action 13–14 *He'll . . . answer* he'll ignore injuries that require him to retaliate

Which tie him to an answer. Our wishes on the way
15 May prove effects. Back, Edmund, to my brother.
16 Hasten his musters and conduct his pow'rs.
17 I must change names at home, and give the distaff
Into my husband's hands. This trusty servant
19 Shall pass between us. Ere long you are like to hear
20 (If you dare venture in your own behalf)
21 A mistress's command. Wear this. Spare speech.
   [Gives a favor.]
Decline your head. This kiss, if it durst speak,
Would stretch thy spirits up into the air.
24 Conceive, and fare thee well.

EDMUND
25 Yours in the ranks of death.   *Exit.*

GONERIL   My most dear Gloucester.
O, the difference of man and man:
To thee a woman's services are due;
28 My fool usurps my body.

OSWALD   Madam, here comes my lord.

                                              [Exit.]

   Enter Albany.

GONERIL
30 I have been worth the whistle.

ALBANY   O Goneril,
You are not worth the dust which the rude wind
Blows in your face. [I fear your disposition:
33 That nature which contemns its origin
34 Cannot be bordered certain in itself.

------

15 *prove effects* be fulfilled; *brother* brother-in-law, Cornwall   16 *musters* the
muster of his troops; *conduct . . . pow'rs* guide his forces   17 *names* roles 17–
18 *give . . . hands* give my husband the housewife's spinning staff   19 *like*
likely   21 *Wear this* (Goneril gives Edmund a lover's token, such as a hand-
kerchief or a glove)   24 *Conceive* understand me   25 *in the ranks of* even up
to   28 *My . . . body* i.e., my idiot husband wrongfully possesses me   30
I . . . whistle "I used to be worth welcoming home," alluding to the proverbial poor dog who is "not worth the whistle"   33 *contemns* despises   34
Cannot . . . certain can have no secure boundaries

She that herself will sliver and disbranch   35
From her material sap, perforce must wither
And come to deadly use.   37

GONERIL
No more; the text is foolish.

ALBANY
Wisdom and goodness to the vile seem vile;
Filths savor but themselves. What have you done?   40
Tigers not daughters, what have you performed? *play vs. reality*
A father, and a gracious agèd man,
Whose reverence even the head-lugged bear would lick,   43
Most barbarous, most degenerate, have you madded.   44
Could my good brother suffer you to do it?   45
A man, a prince, by him so benefited!
If that the heavens do not their visible spirits
Send quickly down to tame these vile offenses,
It will come,
Humanity must perforce prey on itself,   50
Like monsters of the deep.]   51

GONERIL   Milk-livered man,
That bear'st a cheek for blows, a head for wrongs;   52
Who hast not in thy brows an eye discerning   53
Thine honor from thy suffering; [that not know'st
Fools do those villains pity who are punished   55
Ere they have done their mischief. Where's thy drum?   56
France spreads his banners in our noiseless land,   57
With plumèd helm thy state begins to threat,]   58

---

35 *sliver and disbranch* cut herself off and split away   37 *deadly use* destruc-
tiveness   43 *head-lugged* dragged by a chain around its neck (and thus ill-
tempered)   44 *madded* driven mad   45 *brother* brother-in-law   51
Milk-livered cowardly   52 *for* fit for   53–54 *discerning . . . suffering* that can
distinguish what affects your honor (and thus must be resisted) from what
must be endured   55 *Fools* i.e., only fools   56 *drum* i.e., why are you not
mustering your army?   57 *France* the King of France; *noiseless* silent (without the sound of military drums)   58 *thy . . . threat* begins to threaten thy
state (a famous crux, much emended)

59   Whilst thou, a moral fool, sits still and cries
60   "Alack, why does he so?"]
      ALBANY   See thyself, devil:
62   Proper deformity seems not in the fiend
      So horrid as in woman.
      GONERIL   .   O vain fool!
      [ALBANY
63   Thou changèd and self-covered thing, for shame
64   Bemonster not thy feature. Were't my fitness
65   To let these hands obey my blood,
      They are apt enough to dislocate and tear
67   Thy flesh and bones. Howe'er thou art a fiend,
      A woman's shape doth shield thee.
      GONERIL
69   Marry, your manhood – mew!]
            Enter a Messenger.
70   [ALBANY   What news?]
      MESSENGER
      O, my good lord, the Duke of Cornwall's dead,
      Slain by his servant, going to put out
      The other eye of Gloucester.
      ALBANY   Gloucester's eyes?
      MESSENGER
74   A servant that he bred, thrilled with remorse,
      Opposed against the act, bending his sword
      To his great master; who, thereat enraged,
      Flew on him, and amongst them felled him dead;
      But not without that harmful stroke which since
      Hath plucked him after.
      ALBANY   This shows you are above,
80   You justicers, that these our nether crimes

---

59 *moral* moralizing   62 *Proper . . . not* a deformed nature does not appear
62 *vain* silly, worthless   63 *self-covered* hiding your true nature   64
Were't . . . fitness if it were appropriate for me   65 *blood* passion   67 *Howe'er*
although   69 *Marry . . . mew* lock up your manhood; marry = an interjec-
tion, originally an oath on the name of the Virgin Mary   74 *thrilled . . .*
remorse overwhelmed with pity   80 *justicers* (heavenly) judges

So speedily can venge. But, O poor Gloucester,
Lost he his other eye? ↪ *doesn't care about Cornwall*
MESSENGER   Both, both, my lord.
This letter, madam, craves a speedy answer.
'Tis from your sister.
GONERIL *[Aside]*   One way I like this well;
But being widow, and my Gloucester with her,   85
May all the building in my fancy pluck   86
Upon my hateful life. Another way   87
The news is not so tart. – I'll read, and answer. *[Exit.]* 88
ALBANY
Where was his son when they did take his eyes?
MESSENGER
Come with my lady hither.   90
ALBANY   He is not here.
MESSENGER
No, my good lord; I met him back again.   91
ALBANY
Knows he the wickedness?
MESSENGER
Ay, my good lord. 'Twas he informed against him,
And quit the house on purpose, that their punishment
Might have the freer course.
ALBANY   Gloucester, I live
To thank thee for the love thou show'dst the king,
And to revenge thine eyes. Come hither, friend.
Tell me what more thou know'st.   *Exeunt.*

*

❧ **IV.3** *[Enter Kent [disguised] and a Gentleman.*

KENT   Why the King of France is so suddenly gone back
        know you no reason?

---

85 *being* she being   86 *all . . . pluck* pull down my dream-castles   87 *Another way* (i.e., returning to the "one way" of l. 84)   88 *tart* distasteful   91 *back* returning
IV.3 Near Dover

3 GENTLEMAN   Something he left imperfect in the state,
4   which since his coming forth is thought of, which im-
    ports to the kingdom so much fear and danger that his
    personal return was most required and necessary.
KENT
Who hath he left behind him general?
GENTLEMAN   The marshal of France, Monsieur La Far.
KENT   Did your letters pierce the queen to any demon-
10   stration of grief?
GENTLEMAN
Ay, sir. She took them, read them in my presence,
And now and then an ample tear trilled down
Her delicate cheek. It seemed she was a queen
Over her passion, who, most rebel-like,
Sought to be king o'er her.
KENT   O, then it moved her?
GENTLEMAN
Not to a rage. Patience and sorrow strove
17   Who should express her goodliest. You have seen
Sunshine and rain at once – her smiles and tears
19   Were like, a better way: those happy smilets
20   That played on her ripe lip seemed not to know
What guests were in her eyes, which parted thence
As pearls from diamonds dropped. In brief,
23   Sorrow would be a rarity most belovèd,
24   If all could so become it.
KENT   Made she no verbal question?
GENTLEMAN
Faith, once or twice she heaved the name of father
Pantingly forth, as if it pressed her heart;
Cried "Sisters, sisters, shame of ladies, sisters!
Kent, father, sisters? What, i' th' storm, i' th' night?

---

3 *imperfect* incomplete   4–5 *imports* threatens   17 *Who . . . goodliest* which
should best express her feelings   19 *like . . . way* like that, only better   23
rarity jewel   24 *all . . . it* everyone wore it so well

Let pity not be believed!" There she shook   30
The holy water from her heavenly eyes,
And clamor moistened; then away she started   32
To deal with grief alone.
KENT   It is the stars,
The stars above us govern our conditions;
Else one self mate and make could not beget   35
Such different issues. You spoke not with her since?   36
GENTLEMAN   No.
KENT
Was this before the king returned?
GENTLEMAN   No, since.
KENT
Well, sir, the poor distressèd Lear's i' th' town;
Who sometime, in his better tune, remembers   40
What we are come about, and by no means
Will yield to see his daughter.
GENTLEMAN   Why, good sir?
KENT
A sovereign shame so elbows him; his own unkindness,
That stripped her from his benediction, turned her
To foreign casualties, gave her dear rights   45
To his dog-hearted daughters – these things sting
His mind so venomously that burning shame
Detains him from Cordelia.
GENTLEMAN   Alack, poor gentleman.
KENT
Of Albany's and Cornwall's powers you heard not?   50
GENTLEMAN   'Tis so; they are afoot.

---

30 *Let . . . believed* never trust in pity; or, how can pity be believed to exist?
32 *clamor moistened* moistened her grief with tears **35** *one . . . make* one
married couple ("mate" and "make" both mean spouse) **36** *issues* offspring
40 *better tune* more rational state **45** *casualties* dangers; *dear* valuable **50**
powers forces

KENT
    Well, sir, I'll bring you to our master Lear
53   And leave you to attend him. Some dear cause
    Will in concealment wrap me up awhile.
55   When I am known aright, you shall not grieve
    Lending me this acquaintance. I pray you go
    Along with me.   *Exeunt.*]

*

∾ **IV.4** *Enter, with Drum and Colors, Cordelia,*
Gentlemen, [Doctor], and Soldiers.

CORDELIA
    Alack, 'tis he! Why, he was met even now
    As mad as the vexed sea, singing aloud,
3   Crowned with rank fumiter and furrow weeds,
    With hardocks, hemlock, nettles, cuckooflow'rs,
5   Darnel, and all the idle weeds that grow
6   In our sustaining corn. A century send forth!
    Search every acre in the high-grown field
8   And bring him to our eye.   *[Exit an Officer.]*
                      What can man's wisdom
    In the restoring his bereavèd sense?
10   He that helps him take all my outward worth.
DOCTOR
    There is means, madam.
12   Our foster nurse of nature is repose,
13   The which he lacks. That to provoke in him
14   Are many simples operative, whose power
    Will close the eye of anguish.

---

53 *dear* important 55 *grieve* regret
   IV.4 The French camp near Dover 3 *fumiter* fumitory; this, and the following, are all field weeds 5 *idle* useless; uncultivated 6 *sustaining corn*
life-sustaining wheat; *century* troop of one hundred soldiers 8 *What . . .*
wisdom whatever man's wisdom can do 10 *outward worth* material possessions 12 *Our . . . nature* what naturally cares for us 13 *provoke* induce
14 *simples operative* herbal remedies

CORDELIA   All blessed secrets,
  All you unpublished virtues of the earth,   16
  Spring with my tears; be aidant and remediate   17
  In the good man's distress. Seek, seek for him,
  Lest his ungoverned rage dissolve the life
  That wants the means to lead it.   20
      Enter Messenger.
MESSENGER   News, madam.
  The British pow'rs are marching hitherward.
CORDELIA
  'Tis known before. Our preparation stands
  In expectation of them. O dear father,
  · It is thy business that I go about.
  Therefore great France   25
  My mourning, and importuned tears hath pitied.   26
  No blown ambition doth our arms incite,   27
  But love, dear love, and our aged father's right.
  Soon may I hear and see him!   *Exeunt.*
                        *

❧ **IV.5** *Enter Regan and Steward [Oswald].*

REGAN
  But are my brother's pow'rs set forth?   1
OSWALD   Ay, madam.
REGAN
  Himself in person there?
OSWALD
  Madam, with much ado.   4
  Your sister is the better soldier.
REGAN
  Lord Edmund spake not with your lord at home?
OSWALD   No, madam.

---

16 *unpublished virtues* secret powers 17 *be . . . remediate* aid and heal 20
wants lacks 25 *France* the King of France 26 *importuned* importuning
27 *blown* presumptuous
    IV.5 Gloucester's house 1 *brother's pow'rs* Albany's forces 4 *ado* diffi-
culty

REGAN
    What might import my sister's letter to him?
OSWALD   I know not, lady.
REGAN
10   Faith, he is posted hence on serious matter.
    It was great ignorance, Gloucester's eyes being out,
    To let him live. Where he arrives he moves
    All hearts against us. Edmund, I think, is gone,
    In pity of his misery, to dispatch
15   His nighted life; moreover, to descry
    The strength o' th' enemy.
OSWALD
    I must needs after him, madam, with my letter.
REGAN
    Our troops set forth tomorrow. Stay with us.
    The ways are dangerous.
OSWALD   I may not, madam.
20   My lady charged my duty in this business.
REGAN
    Why should she write to Edmund? Might not you
22   Transport her purposes by word? Belike,
    Some things – I know not what. I'll love thee much,
    Let me unseal the letter.
OSWALD   Madam, I had rather –
REGAN
    I know your lady does not love her husband,
27   I am sure of that; and at her late being here
28   She gave strange eliads and most speaking looks
29   To noble Edmund. I know you are of her bosom.
OSWALD   I, madam?
REGAN
31   I speak in understanding – you're, I know't.

---

10 *is posted hence* rushed away from here   15 *nighted* both benighted and
blind; *descry* spy out   20 *charged* strictly commanded   22 *Belike* perhaps
27 *late* recently   28 *eliads* amorous glances   29 *of . . . bosom* in her confi-
dence, with a sexual overtone   31 *understanding* certain knowledge

Therefore I do advise you take this note: 32
My lord is dead; Edmund and I have talked,
And more convenient is he for my hand   34
Than for your lady's. You may gather more.   35
If you do find him, pray you give him this;   36
And when your mistress hears thus much from you,
I pray desire her call her wisdom to her.   38
So fare you well.
If you do chance to hear of that blind traitor,   40
Preferment falls on him that cuts him off.   41

OSWALD
Would I could meet him, madam! I should show
What party I do follow.

REGAN   Fare thee well.   *Exeunt.*

✳

∾ **IV.6**   *Enter Gloucester and Edgar.*

GLOUCESTER
When shall I come to th' top of that same hill?
EDGAR
You do climb up it now. Look how we labor.
GLOUCESTER
Methinks the ground is even.
EDGAR   Horrible steep.
Hark, do you hear the sea?
GLOUCESTER   No, truly.
EDGAR
Why, then, your other senses grow imperfect
By your eyes' anguish.

---

32 *take . . . note* take note of this   34 *convenient* appropriate   35 *gather more* infer more (from what I say)   36 *this* (Perhaps a token; perhaps a letter: Edgar finds only Goneril's letter in Oswald's pockets in IV.6.258, but Oswald, dying, speaks of "letters," so perhaps Edgar misses one. "Letters," on the other hand, could be singular.)   38 *wisdom to her* back to reason   41 *cuts him off* cuts short his life
     IV.6 Open country near Dover

GLOUCESTER   So may it be indeed.
Methinks thy voice is altered, and thou speak'st
In better phrase and matter than thou didst.

EDGAR
You're much deceived. In nothing am I changed
10   But in my garments.

GLOUCESTER   Methinks you're better spoken.

EDGAR
Come on, sir; here's the place. Stand still. How fearful
And dizzy 'tis to cast one's eyes so low!
13   The crows and choughs that wing the midway air
14   Show scarce so gross as beetles. Halfway down
15   Hangs one that gathers samphire – dreadful trade;
Methinks he seems no bigger than his head.
The fishermen that walk upon the beach
18   Appear like mice; and yond tall anchoring bark,
19   Diminished to her cock; her cock, a buoy
20   Almost too small for sight. The murmuring surge
21   That on th' unnumb'red idle pebble chafes
Cannot be heard so high. I'll look no more,
Lest my brain turn, and the deficient sight
24   Topple down headlong.

GLOUCESTER   Set me where you stand.

EDGAR
Give me your hand. You are now within a foot
Of th' extreme verge. For all beneath the moon
27   Would I not leap upright.

GLOUCESTER   Let go my hand.
Here, friend, 's another purse; in it a jewel
Well worth a poor man's taking. Fairies and gods

---

13 *choughs* jackdaws; pronounced "chuffs"   14 *Show* appear; *gross* large   15
samphire Saint Peter's herb, used in pickling; it grows on steep cliffs, hence
the danger in gathering it   18 *bark* ship   19 *cock* dinghy   21 *unnumb'-red . . . pebble* barren reach of innumerable pebbles   24 *Topple* topple me
27 *leap upright* jump upward (to jump forward would reveal to Gloucester
that he is not on the edge of a cliff)

Prosper it with thee. Go thou further off;   30
Bid me farewell, and let me hear thee going.
EDGAR
Now fare ye well, good sir.
GLOUCESTER   With all my heart.
EDGAR   *[Aside]*
Why I do trifle thus with his despair
Is done to cure it.
GLOUCESTER   O you mighty gods!
    [He kneels.]   ↖
This world I do renounce, and in your sights
Shake patiently my great affliction off.
If I could bear it longer and not fall
To quarrel with your great opposeless wills,
My snuff and loathèd part of nature should   39
Burn itself out. If Edgar live, O bless him!   40
Now, fellow, fare thee well.
    [He falls forward and swoons.]
EDGAR   Gone, sir – farewell.
And yet I know not how conceit may rob   42
The treasury of life when life itself
Yields to the theft. Had he been where he thought,   44
By this had thought been past. Alive or dead?   45
Ho you, sir! Friend! Hear you, sir? Speak!
Thus might he pass indeed. Yet he revives.   47
What are you, sir?
GLOUCESTER   Away, and let me die.
EDGAR
Hadst thou been aught but gossamer, feathers, air,   49
So many fathom down precipitating,   50
Thou'dst shivered like an egg; but thou dost breathe, 51

---

30 *Prosper* increase   39 *snuff* burnt-out candle end; *loathèd* ... *nature* despised remnant of life   42 *conceit* illusion, imagination   44 *Yields to* accedes to, welcomes   45 *this* this time   47 *pass indeed* really die   49 *aught* anything   51 *shivered* shattered

Hast heavy substance, bleed'st not, speak'st, art sound.

53 Ten masts at each make not the altitude
Which thou hast perpendicularly fell.
Thy life's a miracle. Speak yet again.

GLOUCESTER
But have I fall'n, or no?

EDGAR
57 From the dread summit of this chalky bourn.
58 Look up a-height. The shrill-gorged lark so far
Cannot be seen or heard. Do but look up.

GLOUCESTER
60 Alack, I have no eyes.
61 Is wretchedness deprived that benefit
To end itself by death? 'Twas yet some comfort
63 When misery could beguile the tyrant's rage
And frustrate his proud will.

EDGAR   Give me your arm.
Up – so. How is't? Feel you your legs? You stand.

GLOUCESTER
Too well, too well.

EDGAR   ,   This is above all strangeness.
Upon the crown o' th' cliff what thing was that
Which parted from you?

GLOUCESTER   A poor unfortunate beggar.

EDGAR
As I stood here below, methought his eyes
70 Were two full moons; he had a thousand noses,
71 Horns whelked and waved like the enridgèd sea.
72 It was some fiend. Therefore, thou happy father,
73 Think that the clearest gods, who make them honors
Of men's impossibilities, have preservèd thee.

---

53 *at each* placed end to end   57 *chalky bourn* chalk cliff, the White Cliffs of
Dover   58 *shrill-gorged* shrill-voiced   61 *deprived* denied   63 *beguile* cheat
71 *whelked* twisted   72 *happy father* lucky old man   73 *clearest* wisest, most
glorious 73–74 *who . . . impossibilities* whose glory consists in performing
miracles

[marginal notes: art vs. nature; moment of theater; edgar transforms again]

GLOUCESTER *changed*
I do remember now. Henceforth I'll bear
Affliction till it do cry out itself
"Enough, enough," and die. That thing you speak of,
I took it for a man. Often 'twould say
"The fiend, the fiend" – he led me to that place.

EDGAR
Bear free and patient thoughts.   80
    Enter Lear [mad, bedecked with weeds].
                              But who comes here?
The safer sense will ne'er accommodate   81
His master thus.

LEAR No, they cannot touch me for coining; I am the   83
king himself.

EDGAR
O thou side-piercing sight!

LEAR Nature's above art in that respect. There's your   86
press money. That fellow handles his bow like a crow-   87
keeper. Draw me a clothier's yard. Look, look, a mouse!   88
Peace, peace; this piece of toasted cheese will do't.   89
There's my gauntlet; I'll prove it on a giant. Bring up   90
the brown bills. O, well flown, bird. I' th' clout, i' th'   91
clout – hewgh! Give the word.   92

EDGAR Sweet marjoram.

LEAR Pass.

GLOUCESTER I know that voice.

---

81 *The . . . sense* a sane mind; *accommodate* array 83 *touch* arrest; *coining* counterfeiting (because minting money was a royal prerogative) 86 *Nature . . . respect* i.e., kings are born, not made 87 *press money* payment for volunteering or being drafted to fight: Lear is conscripting an imaginary army; *crow-keeper* scarecrow 88 *Draw . . . yard* draw the bow out fully (a clothier's yard, 37 inches, was the length of an arrow) 89 *do't* catch the mouse 90 *gauntlet* armored glove (thrown down as a challenge); *prove it on* uphold my cause against 91 *brown bills* pike carriers: Lear continues to assemble his army; *bird* arrow; *clout* bull's-eye 92 *word* password

LEAR   Ha! Goneril with a white beard? They flattered me
97   like a dog, and told me I had the white hairs in my
beard ere the black ones were there. To say "ay" and
99   "no" to everything that I said! "Ay" and "no" too was no
100   good divinity. When the rain came to wet me once, and
the wind to make me chatter; when the thunder would
102   not peace at my bidding; there I found 'em, there I
smelt 'em out. Go to, they are not men o' their words.
They told me I was everything. 'Tis a lie – I am not
105   ague-proof.
GLOUCESTER
106   The trick of that voice I do well remember.
Is't not the king?
LEAR   Ay, every inch a king.
When I do stare, see how the subject quakes.
109   I pardon that man's life. What was thy cause?
110   Adultery?
Thou shalt not die. Die for adultery? No.
The wren goes to't, and the small gilded fly
Does lecher in my sight. *we are just copulating*
Let copulation thrive; for Gloucester's bastard son ⌐ *mean*
Was kinder to his father than my daughters
116   Got 'tween the lawful sheets.
117   To't, luxury, pell-mell, for I lack soldiers.
Behold yond simp'ring dame,
119   Whose face between her forks presages snow,
120   That minces virtue, and does shake the head
To hear of pleasure's name.
122   The fitchew nor the soilèd horse goes to't
With a more riotous appetite.

---

97 *like a dog* as a dog does – i.e., they fawned on me; *the . . . beard* i.e., the
wisdom of age   99–100 *no . . . divinity* bad theology   102 *found 'em* found
them out   105 *ague-proof* immune to fever   106 *trick* special quality   109
cause offense   116 *Got* begotten   117 *luxury* lechery   119 *face . . . forks*
both her face between the combs that hold her hair in place, and her genitals
between her forked legs; *snow* sexual coldness, frigidity   120 *minces* affects
122 *fitchew* both polecat and prostitute; *soilèd* pastured, well-fed

Down from the waist they are centaurs,   124
Though women all above.
But to the girdle do the gods inherit,   126
Beneath is all the fiend's.
There's hell, there's darkness, there is the sulphurous
pit; burning, scalding, stench, consumption. Fie, fie,
fie! pah, pah! Give me an ounce of civet; good apothe-   130
cary, sweeten my imagination! There's money for thee.

GLOUCESTER   O, let me kiss that hand.

LEAR   Let me wipe it first; it smells of mortality.

GLOUCESTER

O ruined piece of nature; this great world   134
Shall so wear out to naught. Dost thou know me?   135

LEAR   I remember thine eyes well enough. Dost thou
squiny at me? No, do thy worst, blind Cupid; I'll not   137
love. Read thou this challenge; mark but the penning
of it.

GLOUCESTER

Were all thy letters suns, I could not see.   140

EDGAR   [Aside]

I would not take this from report – it is,   141
And my heart breaks at it.

LEAR   Read.

GLOUCESTER   What, with the case of eyes?   144

LEAR   O, ho, are you there with me? No eyes in your   145
head, nor no money in your purse? Your eyes are in a
heavy case, your purse in a light; yet you see how this   147
world goes.

GLOUCESTER   I see it feelingly.

---

124 *centaurs* (the classical centaurs were men to the waist and horses below,
and were notoriously lustful)   126 *But . . . girdle* only down to the waist; *inherit* possess   130 *civet* perfume   134 *piece* masterpiece   135 *so . . . naught*
decay to nothing in the same way   137 *squiny* squint   141 *take* believe; *is* is
actually happening   144 *case* sockets   145 *are . . . me* is that what you mean
(with an overtone of "Are we both blind?")   147 *heavy case* sad situation

150 LEAR What, art mad? A man may see how this world
goes with no eyes. Look with thine ears. See how yond
152 justice rails upon yond simple thief. Hark in thine ear:
153 change places and, handy-dandy, which is the justice,
which is the thief? Thou hast seen a farmer's dog bark at
a beggar?

GLOUCESTER Ay, sir.

157 LEAR And the creature run from the cur. There thou
mightst behold the great image of authority – a dog's
159 obeyed in office.

160 Thou rascal beadle, hold thy bloody hand!
Why dost thou lash that whore? Strip thy own back.
162 Thou hotly lusts to use her in that kind
163 For which thou whip'st her. The usurer hangs the cozener.

Through tattered clothes small vices do appear;
165 Robes and furred gowns hide all. Plate sin with gold,
And the strong lance of justice hurtless breaks;
Arm it in rags, a pygmy's straw does pierce it.
168 None does offend, none – I say none! I'll able 'em.
169 Take that of me, my friend, who have the power
170 To seal th' accuser's lips. Get thee glass eyes
171 And, like a scurvy politician, seem
To see the things thou dost not. Now, now, now, now!
Pull off my boots. Harder, harder! So.

EDGAR
174 O, matter and impertinency mixed;
Reason in madness.

---

152 *simple* mere   153 *handy-dandy* the child's game "choose a hand"   157 *creature* man   159 *in office* in a position of power   160 *beadle* church constable   162 *kind* way   163 *usurer . . . cozener* i.e., the big thief hangs the little one; usurer = moneylender, cozener = cheat   165 *Plate . . . gold* cover sin in golden armor   169 *able 'em* vouch for their innocence   169 *Take . . . me* i.e., I pardon you too   170 *glass eyes* eyeglasses   171 *scurvy politician* vile Machiavel   174 *matter . . . impertinency* sense and nonsense

LEAR

  If thou wilt weep my fortunes, take my eyes.

  I know thee well enough; thy name is Gloucester.

  Thou must be patient. We came crying hither;

  Thou know'st, the first time that we smell the air

  We wawl and cry. I will preach to thee. Mark.　　*180*

GLOUCESTER　　Alack, alack the day.

LEAR

  When we are born, we cry that we are come

  To this great stage of fools. – This' a good block.　*183*

  It were a delicate stratagem to shoe　　　　　　*184*

  A troop of horse with felt. I'll put't in proof,

  And when I have stol'n upon these son-in-laws,

  Then kill, kill, kill, kill, kill, kill!　　*volatility*

    Enter a Gentleman [with Attendants].

GENTLEMAN

  O, here he is! Lay hand upon him. – Sir,

  Your most dear daughter –

LEAR

  No rescue? What, a prisoner? I am even　　　　*190*

  The natural fool of fortune. Use me well;　　　*191*

  You shall have ransom. Let me have surgeons;

  I am cut to th' brains.

GENTLEMAN　　　　　　You shall have anything.

LEAR

  No seconds? All myself?　　　　　　　　*194*

  Why, this would make a man a man of salt,　　*195*

  To use his eyes for garden waterpots,　　　　*196*

  [Ay, and laying autumn's dust.] I will die bravely,　*197*

---

183 *This'* this is; *block* felt hat: either the hat decked with weeds, which he removes to begin his sermon, or an imaginary hat suggested by the crown of weeds　**184** *delicate* subtle **184–85** *shoe . . . felt* (and thus enable them to approach silently)　**191** *natural fool* born plaything; *Use* treat　**194** *seconds* supporters　**195** *salt* tears　**196** *waterpots* watering cans　**197** *die* with a quibble on the sexual sense, have an orgasm; *bravely* both courageously and handsomely

198 Like a smug bridegroom. What, I will be jovial!
     Come, come, I am a king; masters, know you that?
GENTLEMAN
200 You are a royal one, and we obey you.
201 LEAR   Then there's life in't. Come, an you get it, you shall
202 get it by running. Sa, sa, sa, sa!
                         Exit [running, followed by Attendants].
GENTLEMAN
     A sight most pitiful in the meanest wretch,
     Past speaking of in a king. Thou hast one daughter
205 Who redeems nature from the general curse
     Which twain have brought her to.   *Cordelia = redemptive force*
EDGAR
207 Hail, gentle sir.
GENTLEMAN   Sir, speed you. What's your will?
EDGAR
208 Do you hear aught, sir, of a battle toward?
GENTLEMAN
209 Most sure and vulgar. Every one hears that
210 Which can distinguish sound.
EDGAR   But, by your favor,
     How near's the other army?
GENTLEMAN
     Near and on speedy foot. The main descry
213 Stands on the hourly thought.
EDGAR   I thank you, sir. That's all.
GENTLEMAN
215 Though that the queen on special cause is here,
     Her army is moved on.

---

198 *smug* neat; satisfied   201 *there's . . . in't* i.e., there's still hope; *an* if   202
sa a hunting cry   205–6 *general . . . to* the universal disruption caused by
your other two daughters; but also, the original sin caused by the filial ingratitude of the original pair, Adam and Eve   207 *gentle* noble; *speed* God
prosper   208 *toward* impending   209 *vulgar* common knowledge   210
Which who   213 *the . . . thought* the sight of the main body is expected
hourly   215 *Though that* however; *on . . . cause* for a particular reason

EDGAR   I thank you, sir. *Exit [Gentleman].*

GLOUCESTER
  You ever-gentle gods, take my breath from me;
  Let not my worser spirit tempt me again   218
  To die before you please.   219

EDGAR   Well pray you, father.

GLOUCESTER
  Now, good sir, what are you?   220

EDGAR
  A most poor man, made tame to fortune's blows,   221
  Who, by the art of known and feeling sorrows,   222
  Am pregnant to good pity. Give me your hand;   223
  I'll lead you to some biding.   224

GLOUCESTER   Hearty thanks.
  The bounty and the benison of heaven   225
  To boot, and boot.   226
      Enter Steward [Oswald].

OSWALD   A proclaimed prize! Most happy;
  That eyeless head of thine was first framed flesh   227
  To raise my fortunes. Thou old unhappy traitor,
  Briefly thyself remember. The sword is out   229
  That must destroy thee.   230

GLOUCESTER   Now let thy friendly hand
  Put strength enough to't.
      [Edgar interposes.]

OSWALD   Wherefore, bold peasant,
  Dar'st thou support a published traitor? Hence,   232
  Lest that th' infection of his fortune take
  Like hold on thee. Let go his arm.

---

218 *worser spirit* "bad side"   219 *father* old man   221 *tame* submissive
222 *art . . . sorrows* lesson of sorrows experienced and deeply felt   223 *pregnant* prone   224 *biding* dwelling   225–26 *bounty . . . boot* may it bring you
the bounty and blessing of heaven, and a reward in addition   226 *proclaimed prize* criminal with a price on his head; *happy* lucky   227 *framed flesh* made human   229 *thyself remember* i.e., remember your sins and pray
232 *published* proclaimed

EDGAR

235   Chill not let go, zir, without vurther 'casion.

OSWALD

Let go, slave, or thou diest.

237 EDGAR   Good gentleman, go your gait, and let poor voke
238   pass. An chud ha' bin zwaggered out of my life, 'twould
not ha' bin zo long as 'tis by a vortnight. Nay, come not
240   near th' old man. Keep out, che vore ye, or Ise try
241   whether your costard or my ballow be the harder. Chill
be plain with you.

OSWALD   Out, dunghill!
        [They fight.]

244 EDGAR   Chill pick your teeth, zir. Come. No matter vor
245   your foins.
        [Oswald falls.]

OSWALD

Slave, thou hast slain me. Villain, take my purse.
If ever thou wilt thrive, bury my body,
248   And give the letters which thou find'st about me
To Edmund Earl of Gloucester. Seek him out
250   Upon the English party. O, untimely death!
Death!
        [He dies.]

EDGAR

I know thee well. A serviceable villain,
As duteous to the vices of thy mistress
As badness would desire.

GLOUCESTER   What, is he dead?

---

235 *Chill* I'll: Edgar adopts a west country dialect; *'casion* occasion, cause
237 *go your gait* be on your way   238 *An . . . zwaggered* if I could have been
bullied   240 *che vore ye* I warn you   241 *your . . . ballow* your head or my
cudgel   244 *pick . . . teeth* i.e., with my club   245 *foins* sword thrusts   248
letters Oswald has a letter for Edmund from Goneril; if he has indeed been
given one by Regan, too, as is implied at IV.5.36, Edgar fails to find it. But
"letters" may be singular (the letters that together compose one letter), as at
I.5.1 250 *Upon* among

EDGAR
Sit you down, father; rest you.
Let's see these pockets; the letters that he speaks of
May be my friends. He's dead; I am only sorry
He had no other deathsman. Let us see.
Leave, gentle wax and manners: blame us not   259
To know our enemies' minds. We rip their hearts;   260
Their papers is more lawful.   261
    Reads the letter.
"Let our reciprocal vows be remembered. You have
many opportunities to cut him off. If your will want   263
not, time and place will be fruitfully offered. There is   264
nothing done, if he return the conqueror. Then am I the   265
prisoner, and his bed my jail; from the loathed warmth
whereof deliver me, and supply the place for your labor.   267
    "Your (wife, so I would say) affectionate servant,
                                              "Goneril."

O indistinguished space of woman's will –   270
A plot upon her virtuous husband's life,
And the exchange my brother! Here in the sands
Thee I'll rake up, the post unsanctified   273
Of murderous lechers; and in the mature time   274
With this ungracious paper strike the sight
Of the death-practiced duke. For him 'tis well   276
That of thy death and business I can tell.   277
GLOUCESTER
The king is mad. How stiff is my vile sense,   278

---

259 *Leave . . . wax* by your leave, kind seal   261 *Their* to rip their   263 *him*
Albany; *If . . . not* if you do not lack the will   264 *fruitfully* i.e., promising
success   265 *done* accomplished   267 *supply* fill   270 *indistinguished* un-
limited   273 *rake up* cover over; *post unsanctified* unholy messenger   274
in . . . time when the time is ripe   276 *death-practiced* whose death is plotted
277 (None of the original texts makes any provision for the removal of Oswald's body. Editors since the eighteenth century have had Edgar exit here
dragging it offstage, and then return six lines later. The very awkward alternative is for him to remove it while he is also leading Gloucester offstage.)
278 *How . . . sense* how obstinate is my hateful consciousness

279   That I stand up, and have ingenious feeling
280   Of my huge sorrows! Better I were distract;
       So should my thoughts be severed from my griefs,
282   And woes by wrong imaginations lose
       The knowledge of themselves.
           Drum afar off.
EDGAR   Give me your hand.
       Far off methinks I hear the beaten drum.
       Come, father, I'll bestow you with a friend.   *Exeunt.*

                              *

∿ **IV.7** *Enter Cordelia, Kent, [Doctor,] and Gentleman.*

CORDELIA
       O thou good Kent, how shall I live and work
       To match thy goodness? My life will be too short
       And every measure fail me.
KENT
4   To be acknowledged, madam, is o'erpaid.
5   All my reports go with the modest truth;
6   Nor more nor clipped, but so.
CORDELIA   Be better suited.
7   These weeds are memories of those worser hours.
       I prithee put them off.
KENT   Pardon, dear madam.
9   Yet to be known shortens my made intent.
10   My boon I make it that you know me not
11   Till time and I think meet.
CORDELIA
       Then be't so, my good lord.
           [To the Doctor]   How does the king?

___

279 *ingenious* rational, intelligent 280 *distract* mad 282 *wrong imaginations* delusions

IV.7 The French camp 4 *o'erpaid* more than sufficient 5 *go* accord 6 *clipped* less; *suited* dressed 7 *weeds* clothes; *memories* reminders 9 *Yet . . . intent* to reveal myself now would spoil my plan (for Lear to recognize him as Kent) 10 *My . . . it* I ask as my reward 11 *meet* suitable

DOCTOR
  Madam, sleeps still.
CORDELIA
  O you kind gods,
  Cure this great breach in his abusèd nature!
  Th' untuned and jarring senses, O, wind up   16
  Of this child-changèd father!   17
DOCTOR
  So please your majesty
  That we may wake the king? He hath slept long.
CORDELIA
  Be governed by your knowledge, and proceed   20
  I' th' sway of your own will. Is he arrayed?   21
    Enter Lear in a chair carried by Servants.
GENTLEMAN
  Ay, madam. In the heaviness of sleep
  We put fresh garments on him.
DOCTOR
  Be by, good madam, when we do awake him.
  I doubt not of his temperance.   25
[CORDELIA   Very well.
    [Music.]
DOCTOR
  Please draw near. Louder the music there.]
CORDELIA
  O my dear father, restoration hang
  Thy medicine on my lips, and let this kiss
  Repair those violent harms that my two sisters
  Have in thy reverence made.   30
KENT   Kind and dear princess.
CORDELIA
  Had you not been their father, these white flakes   31

---

16 *jarring* discordant; *wind up* put in tune   17 *child-changèd* both changed
by his children and changed into a child   21 *I' th' sway . . . will* as you see fit;
arrayed properly dressed   25 *temperance* self-control   30 *in . . . reverence* on
the dignity of your age   31 *flakes* hairs

32   Did challenge pity of them. Was this a face
To be opposed against the jarring winds?
[To stand against the deep dread-bolted thunder?
In the most terrible and nimble stroke
36   Of quick cross lightning to watch, poor perdu,
37   With this thin helm?] Mine enemy's dog,   *Lear = dog,*
Though he had bit me, should have stood that night *animal*
39   Against my fire; and wast thou fain, poor father,
40   To hovel thee with swine and rogues forlorn
41   In short and musty straw? Alack, alack,
'Tis wonder that thy life and wits at once
Had not concluded all. – He wakes. Speak to him.

DOCTOR
Madam, do you; 'tis fittest.

CORDELIA
How does my royal lord? How fares your majesty?

LEAR   *sleep = death*
You do me wrong to take me out o' th' grave.
Thou art a soul in bliss; but I am bound
48   Upon a wheel of fire, that mine own tears *some form of*
Do scald like molten lead.   *punishment*

CORDELIA   Sir, do you know me?

LEAR
50   You are a spirit, I know. Where did you die?

CORDELIA
51   Still, still, far wide!

DOCTOR
He's scarce awake. Let him alone awhile.

LEAR
Where have I been? Where am I? Fair daylight?
54   I am mightily abused. I should e'en die with pity

---

32 *challenge* demand   36 *watch* stand guard; *perdu* an exposed (and expendable) sentry   37 *helm* helmet (i.e., his white hair)   39 *Against* beside; *fain* obliged   41 *short* broken   48 *wheel of fire* the image combines the wheel on which prisoners were bound for beatings with the burning of heretics or of souls in hell   51 *wide* wide of the mark   54 *abused* ill-used, deceived

To see another thus. I know not what to say.
I will not swear these are my hands. Let's see —⌉
I feel this pin prick. Would I were assured   ⌋
Of my condition.

CORDELIA   O look upon me, sir,
And hold your hand in benediction o'er me.
You must not kneel.   *60*

LEAR
Pray, do not mock me.
I am a very foolish fond old man,   *62*
Fourscore and upward, not an hour more nor less;
And, to deal plainly,
I fear I am not in my perfect mind.
Methinks I should know you, and know this man:
Yet I am doubtful, for I am mainly ignorant   *67*
What place this is; and all the skill I have
Remembers not these garments; nor I know not
Where I did lodge last night. Do not laugh at me;   *70*
For, as I am a man, I think this lady
To be my child Cordelia.

CORDELIA   And so I am! I am!

LEAR
Be your tears wet? Yes, faith. I pray weep not.
If you have poison for me, I will drink it.
I know you do not love me; for your sisters
Have (as I do remember) done me wrong.
You have some cause, they have not.

CORDELIA   No cause, no cause.

LEAR
Am I in France?

KENT   In your own kingdom, sir.

LEAR
Do not abuse me.   *80*

DOCTOR
Be comforted, good madam. The great rage

---

62 *fond* (the word also means foolish)   **67** *mainly* entirely   **80** *abuse* deceive

You see is killed in him; [and yet it is danger
83   To make him even o'er the time he has lost.]
Desire him to go in. Trouble him no more
85   Till further settling.
CORDELIA
Will't please your highness walk?
LEAR   You must bear with me.
Pray you now, forget and forgive. I am old and foolish.
                        Exeunt. [Manent Kent and Gentleman.]
[GENTLEMAN   Holds it true, sir, that the Duke of Cornwall was so slain?
90   KENT   Most certain, sir.
91   GENTLEMAN   Who is conductor of his people?
KENT   As 'tis said, the bastard son of Gloucester.
GENTLEMAN   They say Edgar, his banished son, is with
the Earl of Kent in Germany.
95   KENT   Report is changeable. 'Tis time to look about; the
96   powers of the kingdom approach apace.
97   GENTLEMAN   The arbitrament is like to be bloody. Fare
you well, sir.   *[Exit.]*
KENT
99   My point and period will be throughly wrought,
100 Or well or ill, as this day's battle's fought.   *Exit.]*
                                *

∾ **V.1** *Enter, with Drum and Colors, Edmund, Regan,
Gentleman, and Soldiers.*

EDMUND
1   Know of the duke if his last purpose hold,
2   Or whether since he is advised by aught

---

83 *even o'er* fill in   85 *settling* calm sets in   91 *conductor . . . people* com-
mander of his forces   95 *Report* rumor; *look about* see to our preparations
96 *powers* forces   97 *arbitrament* action   99 *My . . . wrought* my purpose
and end will be fully completed   100 *Or* either
  V.1 The British camp   1 *Know . . . hold* find out from Albany if his most
recent intention (to join in the fight against Cordelia's forces) still holds good
2 *since* since then

To change the course. He's full of alteration
And self-reproving. Bring his constant pleasure.   4
[Exit an Officer.]

REGAN
Our sister's man is certainly miscarried.   5

EDMUND
'Tis to be doubted, madam.   6

REGAN   Now, sweet lord,
You know the goodness I intend upon you.
Tell me, but truly – but then speak the truth –
Do you not love my sister?   *haha*   9

EDMUND   In honored love.

REGAN
But have you never found my brother's way   10
To the forfended place?   11

[EDMUND   That thought abuses you.

REGAN
I am doubtful that you have been conjunct   13
And bosomed with her, as far as we call hers.]   14

EDMUND
No, by mine honor, madam.

REGAN
I never shall endure her. Dear my lord,
Be not familiar with her.   17

EDMUND   Fear me not.
She and the duke her husband!
Enter, with Drum and Colors, Albany, Goneril,
Soldiers.

[GONERIL   *[Aside]*
I had rather lose the battle than that sister
Should loosen him and me.]   20

fighting over a lover

———

4 *constant pleasure* firm decision   5 *sister's man* Oswald; *is . . . miscarried* has
certainly met with an accident   6 *doubted* feared   9 *honored* honorable   10
brother's Albany's   11 *forfended* forbidden; *abuses* is unworthy of   13 *doubt-*
ful suspicious   13–14 *conjunct . . . her* both in complicity with her and her
lover   14 *as . . . hers* as completely hers as you can be   17 *familiar* intimate;
fear doubt

ALBANY
    Our very loving sister, well bemet.
    Sir, this I heard: the king is come to his daughter,
23   With others whom the rigor of our state
24   Forced to cry out. [Where I could not be honest,
    I never yet was valiant. For this business,
26   It touches us as France invades our land,
27   Not bolds the king with others, whom I fear
28   Most just and heavy causes make oppose.
EDMUND
29   Sir, you speak nobly.]
REGAN   Why is this reasoned?
GONERIL
30   Combine together 'gainst the enemy;
31   For these domestic and particular broils
32   Are not the question here.
ALBANY   Let's then determine
33   With th' ancient of war on our proceeding.
[EDMUND
    I shall attend you presently at your tent.]
REGAN
    Sister, you'll go with us?
GONERIL   No.
REGAN
37   'Tis most convenient. Pray go with us.
GONERIL
38   O ho, I know the riddle. – I will go.

                              Exeunt both the Armies.
    Enter Edgar.

---

23 *rigor . . . state* harshness of our rule   24 *be honest* behave honorably   26 *touches* concerns   27 *Not bolds* not because he emboldens   28 *heavy* serious   29 *Why . . . reasoned?* i.e., why are you telling us this?   30 *Combine together* let us join our forces   31 *particular broils* private quarrels   32 *question* issue   33 *th' ancient of war* experienced senior officers   37 *convenient* proper that you do   38 *I . . . riddle* I get the point (which is to prevent her from being alone with Edmund)

EDGAR   *[To Albany]*
    If e'er your grace had speech with man so poor,
    Hear me one word.   40

ALBANY   *[To those departing]*
                    I'll overtake you. *[To Edgar]* Speak.

EDGAR
    Before you fight the battle, ope this letter.
    If you have victory, let the trumpet sound
    For him that brought it. Wretched though I seem,
    I can produce a champion that will prove   44
    What is avouchèd there. If you miscarry,   45
    Your business of the world hath so an end,
    And machination ceases. Fortune love you.   47

ALBANY
    Stay till I have read the letter.

EDGAR   I was forbid it.
    When time shall serve, let but the herald cry,
    And I'll appear again.   50

ALBANY
    Why, fare thee well. I will o'erlook thy paper.
                                        Exit [Edgar].

        Enter Edmund.

EDMUND
    The enemy's in view; draw up your powers.
    Here is the guess of their true strength and forces   53
    By diligent discovery; but your haste   54
    Is now urged on you.   55

ALBANY   We will greet the time.   *Exit.*

EDMUND
    To both these sisters have I sworn my love;
    Each jealous of the other, as the stung   57

---

44 *prove* establish as true (in a trial by single combat)   45 *avouchèd* asserted;
miscarry lose the battle   47 *machination* plotting   51 **s.d.** Presumably Albany has no time to read Oswald's letter before Edmund's entrance.   53
guess estimate   54 *discovery* spying   55 *greet the time* be ready when the time
comes   57 *jealous* suspicious; *stung* those who have been bitten

Are of the adder. Which of them shall I take?
Both? One? Or neither? Neither can be enjoyed,
60 If both remain alive. To take the widow
Exasperates, makes mad her sister Goneril;
62 And hardly shall I carry out my side,
Her husband being alive. Now then, we'll use
64 His countenance for the battle, which being done,
Let her who would be rid of him devise
66 His speedy taking off. As for the mercy
Which he intends to Lear and to Cordelia –
The battle done, and they within our power,
69 Shall never see his pardon; for my state
70 Stands on me to defend, not to debate.   *Exit.*

                        *

∾ **V.2** *Alarum within. Enter, with Drum and Colors,*
Lear, [held by the hand by] Cordelia; and Soldiers [of
France], over the stage and exeunt.
Enter Edgar and Gloucester.

EDGAR
1 Here, father, take the shadow of this tree
2 For your good host. Pray that the right may thrive.
If ever I return to you again,
4 I'll bring you comfort.
GLOUCESTER   Grace go with you, sir.
                                    Exit [Edgar].
Alarum and retreat within. Enter Edgar.
EDGAR
Away, old man! Give me thy hand. Away!
King Lear hath lost, he and his daughter ta'en.

---

62 *carry . . . side* accomplish my plan   64 *countenance* authority, backing
66 *taking off* murder   69 *Shall* they shall   69–70 *state . . . me* situation requires me
V.2 A field   s.d. *Alarum within* trumpets offstage   1 *father* old man:
Edgar still has not revealed his identity to Gloucester   2 *host* shelter   4 s.d.
retreat i.e., sound of retreating army

Give me thy hand. Come on.
GLOUCESTER
  No further, sir. A man may rot even here.
EDGAR
  What, in ill thoughts again? Men must endure
  Their going hence, even as their coming hither;   10
  Ripeness is all. Come on.   11
GLOUCESTER   And that's true too.   *Exeunt.*
                        *

∾ **V.3** *Enter, in conquest, with Drum and Colors,*
     Edmund; Lear and Cordelia as prisoners; Soldiers,
     Captain.

EDMUND
  Some officers take them away. Good guard
  Until their greater pleasures first be known   2
  That are to censure them.   3
CORDELIA   We are not the first
  Who with best meaning have incurred the worst.   4
  For thee, oppressèd king, I am cast down;
  Myself could else outfrown false Fortune's frown.   6
  Shall we not see these daughters and these sisters?
LEAR
  No, no, no, no! Come, let's away to prison.   *prison is ok if*
  We two alone will sing like birds i' th' cage.   *they are*
  When thou dost ask me blessing, I'll kneel down   *together*   10
  And ask of thee forgiveness. So we'll live,
  And pray, and sing, and tell old tales, and laugh
  At gilded butterflies, and hear poor rogues
  Talk of court news; and we'll talk with them too –
  Who loses and who wins; who's in, who's out –
  And take upon's the mystery of things

---

11 *Ripeness is all* i.e., the gods decree when fruit is ripe and falls; coming to
that ripeness is all that matters
   V.3 The British camp   2 *their . . . pleasures* the wishes of those in command   3 *censure* pass judgment on   4 *meaning* intentions   6 *else* otherwise

17 As if we were God's spies; and we'll wear out,
18 In a walled prison, packs and sects of great ones
19 That ebb and flow by th' moon.
EDMUND   Take them away.
LEAR
20 Upon such sacrifices, my Cordelia,
21 The gods themselves throw incense. Have I caught thee?
22 He that parts us shall bring a brand from heaven
    And fire us hence like foxes. Wipe thine eyes.
24 The goodyears shall devour them, flesh and fell,
    Ere they shall make us weep! We'll see 'em starved first.
    Come.   *Exeunt [Lear and Cordelia, guarded].*
EDMUND
    Come hither, captain; hark.
    Take thou this note.
        [Gives a paper.]   Go follow them to prison.
28 One step I have advanced thee. If thou dost
    As this instructs thee, thou dost make thy way
30 To noble fortunes. Know thou this, that men
31 Are as the time is. To be tender-minded
32 Does not become a sword. Thy great employment
33 Will not bear question. Either say thou'lt do't,
    Or thrive by other means.
CAPTAIN   I'll do't, my lord.
EDMUND
35 About it; and write happy when thou'st done.
36 Mark, I say instantly, and carry it so
    As I have set it down.

---

17 *wear out* outlast   18 *packs and sects* parties and factions   19 *That . . .
moon* whose power changes monthly   21 *throw incense* are celebrants;
Have . . . thee? i.e., do I really have you again?   22 *brand* torch; i.e., it will
take divine powers to separate us now   24 *goodyears* passage of time, old age;
flesh . . . fell meat and skin, entirely   28 *advanced* promoted   31 *Are . . . is*
i.e., must seize their opportunities   32 *sword* i.e., soldier   33 *question* discussion   35 *write happy* call yourself fortunate   36 *carry it* carry it out

[CAPTAIN
 I cannot draw a cart, nor eat dried oats –   38
 If it be a man's work, I'll do't.]   *Exit.*
         Flourish. Enter Albany, Goneril, Regan, Soldiers.
ALBANY
 Sir, you have showed today your valiant strain,   40
 And fortune led you well. You have the captives
 Who were the opposites of this day's strife.   42
 I do require them of you, so to use them   43
 As we shall find their merits and our safety
 May equally determine.
EDMUND
 Sir, I thought it fit
 To send the old and miserable king
 To some retention [and appointed guard];   48
 Whose age had charms in it, whose title more,
 To pluck the common bosom on his side   50
 And turn our impressed lances in our eyes   51
 Which do command them. With him I sent the queen,
 My reason all the same; and they are ready
 Tomorrow, or at further space, t' appear   54
 Where you shall hold your session. [At this time   55
 We sweat and bleed, the friend hath lost his friend,
 And the best quarrels, in the heat, are cursed   57
 By those that feel their sharpness.   58
 The question of Cordelia and her father
 Requires a fitter place.]   *60*
ALBANY   Sir, by your patience,
 I hold you but a subject of this war,   61
 Not as a brother.   62

---

38 *draw . . . oats* i.e., I'm a man, not a horse   **40** *strain* both qualities and
lineage   **42** *opposites of* opponents in   **43** *use* treat   **48** *retention* detention
50 *pluck . . . on* draw popular sympathy to   **51** *turn . . . eyes* i.e., turn our
soldiers against us; *impressed lances* drafted pikemen   **54** *further space* a later
time   **55** *session* court hearing   **57** *best . . . heat* most just wars in the heat of
battle   **58** *feel . . . sharpness* endure their pain   **61** *subject of* subordinate in

REGAN   That's as we list to grace him.
63   Methinks our pleasure might have been demanded
      Ere you had spoke so far. He led our powers,
65   Bore the commission of my place and person,
66   The which immediacy may well stand up
67   And call itself your brother.
GONERIL   Not so hot!
68   In his own grace he doth exalt himself
69   More than in your addition.
REGAN   .   In my rights
70   By me invested, he compeers the best.
ALBANY
71   That were the most if he should husband you.
REGAN
      Jesters do oft prove prophets.
GONERIL   Holla, holla!
73   That eye that told you so looked but asquint.
REGAN
      Lady, I am not well; else I should answer
75   From a full-flowing stomach. General,
76   Take thou my soldiers, prisoners, patrimony;
77   Dispose of them, of me; the walls is thine.
      Witness the world that I create thee here
      My lord and master.
GONERIL   Mean you to enjoy him?
ALBANY
80   The let-alone lies not in your good will.
EDMUND
81   Nor in thine, lord.

---

62 *we list* I please   63 *pleasure . . . demanded* wishes should have been con-
sulted   65 *Bore . . . person* i.e., acted with my authority   66 *immediacy* present status (as my deputy)   67 *hot* fast   68 *grace* merit   69 *your addition* the
honors conferred by you   70 *compeers* equals   71 *the most* i.e., the most
complete investiture with your rights   73 *asquint* cross-eyed, i.e., jealously
75 *stomach* anger   76 *patrimony* inheritance   77 *the . . . thine* i.e., you have
captured my castle   80 *let-alone* both permission and veto

ALBANY   Half-blooded fellow, yes.

REGAN   *[To Edmund]*

Let the drum strike, and prove my title thine.   82

ALBANY

Stay yet; hear reason. Edmund, I arrest thee
On capital treason; and, in thy attaint,   84
This gilded serpent.
      [Points to Goneril.] For your claim, fair sister,
I bar it in the interest of my wife.
'Tis she is subcontracted to this lord,   87
And I, her husband, contradict your banns.   88
If you will marry, make your loves to me;   89
My lady is bespoke.   90

GONERIL   An interlude!

ALBANY

Thou art armed, Gloucester. Let the trumpet sound.
If none appear to prove upon thy person
Thy heinous, manifest, and many treasons,
There is my pledge.   94
      [Throws down a glove.] I'll make it on thy heart,
Ere I taste bread, thou art in nothing less   95
Than I have here proclaimed thee.

REGAN   Sick, O sick!

GONERIL   *[Aside]*

If not, I'll ne'er trust medicine.   97

EDMUND

There's my exchange.   98
      [Throws down a glove.] What in the world he is
That names me traitor, villainlike he lies.
Call by the trumpet. He that dares approach,   *100*

---

81 *Half-blooded* illegitimate (and only half noble)   82 *drum strike* as a signal
to prepare for battle   84 *in . . . attaint* in complicity with your crimes   87
subcontracted (because she is already contracted, by marriage, to Albany)   88
banns declaration of an intention to marry   89 *make . . . to* woo   90 *bespoke*
already spoken for; *interlude* farce   94 *make* prove   95 *nothing less* no way
less guilty   97 *medicine* i.e., poison   98 *What . . . world* whoever

On him, on you, who not? I will maintain
My truth and honor firmly.

ALBANY
A herald, ho!

[EDMUND   A herald, ho, a herald!]

ALBANY
104 Trust to thy single virtue; for thy soldiers,
All levied in my name, have in my name
Took their discharge.

REGAN   My sickness grows upon me.

ALBANY
She is not well. Convey her to my tent.
                         [Exit Regan, attended.]
     Enter a Herald.
Come hither, herald. Let the trumpet sound,
And read out this.

110 [CAPTAIN   Sound, trumpet!]
     A trumpet sounds.

HERALD   *Reads.* "If any man of quality or degree within
the lists of the army will maintain upon Edmund, supposed Earl of Gloucester, that he is a manifold traitor,
let him appear by the third sound of the trumpet. He is
bold in his defense."

[EDMUND   Sound!]
     First trumpet.

HERALD   Again!
     Second trumpet.

118 Again!
     Third trumpet.
     Trumpet answers within.
     *Enter Edgar, armed [at the third sound, a Trumpeter
     before him].*

---

104 *single virtue* unaided strength   **118 s.d.** *armed* Edgar wears a helmet
with the beaver down, covering his face

ALBANY
Ask him his purposes, why he appears
Upon this call o' th' trumpet.   *120*
HERALD   What are you?
Your name, your quality, and why you answer   *121*
This present summons?
EDGAR   Know my name is lost,
By treason's tooth bare-gnawn and canker-bit;   *123*
Yet am I noble as the adversary
I come to cope. ⤷ *for him, they were always on*₁₂₅
ALBANY   Which is that adversary? *equal footing*
EDGAR
What's he that speaks for Edmund Earl of Gloucester?
EDMUND
Himself. What say'st thou to him?
EDGAR   Draw thy sword.
That, if my speech offend a noble heart,
Thy arm may do thee justice. Here is mine.
Behold it is my privilege,   *130*
The privilege of mine honors,
My oath, and my profession. I protest –   *132*
Maugre thy strength, place, youth, and eminence,   *133*
Despite thy victor sword and fire-new fortune,   *134*
Thy valor and thy heart – thou art a traitor,   *135*
False to thy gods, thy brother, and thy father,
Conspirant 'gainst this high illustrious prince,   *137*
And from th' extremest upward of thy head   *138*
To the descent and dust below thy foot   *139*
A most toad-spotted traitor. Say thou "no,"   *140*
This sword, this arm, and my best spirits are bent

---

121 *quality* rank   123 *treason's* treachery's; *canker-bit* eaten away by worms
125 *cope* encounter   132 *profession* i.e., as a knight   133 *Maugre* despite
134 *fire-new* newly forged   135 *heart* courage   137 *Conspirant* conspirator
138 *upward* top   139 *descent* lowest part   140 *toad-spotted* venomous, rep-
tilian

To prove upon thy heart, whereto I speak,
143 Thou liest.
EDMUND   In wisdom I should ask thy name,
But since thy outside looks so fair and warlike,
145 And that thy tongue some say of breeding breathes,
146 What safe and nicely I might well delay
147 By rule of knighthood I disdain and spurn.
Back do I toss these treasons to thy head,
149 With the hell-hated lie o'erwhelm thy heart,
150 Which – for they yet glance by and scarcely bruise –
151 This sword of mine shall give them instant way
Where they shall rest forever. Trumpets, speak!
        Alarums. Fight. [Edmund falls.]
ALBANY
153 Save him, save him.
GONERIL   This is practice, Gloucester.
By th' law of war thou wast not bound to answer
155 An unknown opposite. Thou art not vanquished,
156 But cozened and beguiled.
ALBANY   Shut your mouth, dame,
Or with this paper shall I stop it. – Hold, sir. –
        [To Goneril]
Thou worse than any name, read thine own evil.
No tearing, lady! I perceive you know it.
GONERIL
160 Say if I do – the laws are mine, not thine.
161 Who can arraign me for't?
ALBANY   Most monstrous! O,
Know'st thou this paper?

---

143 *In . . . name* (because one was not obliged to fight with an inferior, nor
with an unknown adversary)   145 *say* touch, sign   146 *safe and nicely* cau-
tiously and correctly   147 *disdain and spurn* i.e., to ask what I am entitled to
know   149 *hell-hated* hateful as hell   150 *Which – for they* since those treasons   151 *way* access   153 *Save him* i.e., don't kill him; *This is practice* i.e.,
you've been tricked   155 *opposite* opponent   156 *cozened* cheated   160
the . . . mine Goneril is queen; Albany is her consort   161 *arraign* try; the
monarch, having no peers, could not be prosecuted

GONERIL   Ask me not what I know.

                                                    Exit.

ALBANY
  Go after her. She's desperate; govern her.   163

                                        [Exit an Officer.]

EDMUND
  What you have charged me with, that have I done,
  And more, much more. The time will bring it out.
  'Tis past, and so am I. – But what art thou
  That hast this fortune on me? If thou'rt noble,   167
  I do forgive thee. ~~mmic~~   168

EDGAR   Let's exchange charity.
  I am no less in blood than thou art, Edmund;
  If more, the more thou'st wronged me.   *170*
  My name is Edgar and thy father's son.
  The gods are just, and of our pleasant vices   172
  Make instruments to plague us.
  The dark and vicious place where thee he got   174
  Cost him his eyes.

EDMUND   Thou'st spoken right; 'tis true.
  The wheel is come full circle; I am here.   176

ALBANY
  Methought thy very gait did prophesy
  A royal nobleness. I must embrace thee.
  Let sorrow split my heart if ever I
  Did hate thee, or thy father.   *180*

EDGAR   Worthy prince, I know't.

ALBANY
  Where have you hid yourself?
  How have you known the miseries of your father?

EDGAR
  By nursing them, my lord. List a brief tale;   184

---

163 *govern* take care of   167 *fortune on* victory over   168 *charity* forgiveness
172 *pleasant* pleasurable   174 *dark . . . place* adulterous bed, illicit genitals;
got begot   176 *I . . . here* i.e., at the bottom of Fortune's Wheel again   184
List hear

And when 'tis told, O that my heart would burst!
186 The bloody proclamation to escape
187 That followed me so near (O our lives' sweetness,
That we the pain of death would hourly die
Rather than die at once!) taught me to shift
190 Into a madman's rags, t' assume a semblance
That very dogs disdained; and in this habit
192 Met I my father with his bleeding rings,
Their precious stones new lost; became his guide,
Led him, begged for him, saved him from despair;
Never – O fault! – revealed myself unto him
Until some half hour past, when I was armed,
Not sure, though hoping of this good success,
I asked his blessing, and from first to last
Told him our pilgrimage. But his flawed heart –
200 Alack, too weak the conflict to support –
'Twixt two extremes of passion, joy and grief,
Burst smilingly.

EDMUND   This speech of yours hath moved me,
And shall perchance do good; but speak you on –
You look as you had something more to say.

ALBANY
If there be more, more woeful, hold it in,
206 For I am almost ready to dissolve,
207 Hearing of this.

[EDGAR   This would have seemed a period
208 To such as love not sorrow; but another,
To amplify too much, would make much more,
210 And top extremity.
211 Whilst I was big in clamor, came there in a man,
212 Who, having seen me in my worst estate,
Shunned my abhorred society; but then, finding

---

186 *bloody proclamation* (declaring him an outlaw)   187 *our . . . sweetness*
how sweet life is to us   192 *rings* sockets   206 *dissolve* (in tears)   207 *a period* the limit   208–10 *another . . . extremity* to describe another sorrow too
fully would exceed the limit   211 *big in clamor* loudly lamenting   212
in . . . estate at my worst

Who 'twas that so endured, with his strong arms
He fastened on my neck, and bellowed out
As he'd burst heaven, threw him on my father,   216
Told the most piteous tale of Lear and him
That ever ear received; which in recounting
His grief grew puissant, and the strings of life   219
Began to crack. Twice then the trumpets sounded,   220
And there I left him tranced.

ALBANY   But who was this?

EDGAR
Kent, sir, the banished Kent; who in disguise
Followed his enemy king and did him service
Improper for a slave.]
    Enter a Gentleman [with a bloody knife].

GENTLEMAN
Help, help! O, help!

EDGAR   What kind of help?

ALBANY   Speak, man.

EDGAR
What means this bloody knife?

GENTLEMAN   'Tis hot, it smokes.
It came even from the heart of – O, she's dead.

ALBANY
Who dead? Speak, man.   230

GENTLEMAN
Your lady, sir, your lady; and her sister
By her is poisonèd; she confesses it.

EDMUND
I was contracted to them both. All three
Now marry in an instant.   234

EDGAR   Here comes Kent.
    Enter Kent.

ALBANY
Produce the bodies, be they alive or dead.
                              [Exit Gentleman.]

---

216 *As* as if; *him* himself   219 *puissant* powerful   234 *marry* unite

This judgment of the heavens, that makes us tremble,
Touches us not with pity. – O, is this he?
The time will not allow the compliment
Which very manners urges.

KENT   I am come
240   To bid my king and master aye good night.
Is he not here?

ALBANY   Great thing of us forgot!
Speak, Edmund, where's the king? and where's Cordelia?
Goneril and Regan's bodies brought out.
243   Seest thou this object, Kent?

KENT
Alack, why thus?

EDMUND   Yet Edmund was beloved.
The one the other poisoned for my sake,
And after slew herself.

ALBANY
Even so. Cover their faces.   *↗ I'm bad, but I'll do*
                                          a good thing
EDMUND
I pant for life. Some good I mean to do,
Despite of mine own nature. Quickly send –
250   Be brief in it – to th' castle, for my writ
Is on the life of Lear and on Cordelia.
Nay, send in time.

ALBANY   Run, run, O run!

EDGAR
254   To who, my lord? Who has the office? Send
Thy token of reprieve.

EDMUND
Well thought on. Take my sword;
Give it the captain.

EDGAR   Haste thee for thy life. *[Exit Officer.]*

EDMUND
He hath commission from thy wife and me

---

240 *aye* forever   **243** *object* sight, spectacle   **250** *brief* quick; *writ* order of
execution   **254** *office* commission

To hang Cordelia in the prison and
To lay the blame upon her own despair   260
That she fordid herself.   261

ALBANY
The gods defend her! Bear him hence awhile.
                              [Edmund is borne off.]
Enter Lear, with Cordelia in his arms [, Gentleman,
and others following].

LEAR
Howl, howl, howl! O, you are men of stones.
Had I your tongues and eyes, I'd use them so
That heaven's vault should crack. She's gone forever.
I know when one is dead, and when one lives.
She's dead as earth. Lend me a looking glass.
If that her breath will mist or stain the stone,   268
Why then she lives.   269

KENT   Is this the promised end?

EDGAR
Or image of that horror?   270

ALBANY   Fall and cease.

LEAR
This feather stirs; she lives! If it be so,
It is a chance which does redeem all sorrows
That ever I have felt.

KENT   O my good master.

LEAR
Prithee away.

EDGAR   'Tis noble Kent, your friend.

LEAR
A plague upon you murderers, traitors all;
I might have saved her; now she's gone forever.
Cordelia, Cordelia, stay a little. Ha,
What is't thou say'st? Her voice was ever soft,

---

261 *fordid* destroyed   **268** *stone* mirror of polished stone   **269** *promised end*
Judgment Day   **270** *Fall . . . cease* let the world end

Gentle, and low – an excellent thing in woman.
280 I killed the slave that was a-hanging thee.
GENTLEMAN
'Tis true, my lords, he did.
LEAR   Did I not, fellow?
282 I have seen the day, with my good biting falchion
I would have made them skip. I am old now,
284 And these same crosses spoil me. Who are you?
Mine eyes are not o' th' best, I'll tell you straight.
KENT
286 If Fortune brag of two she loved and hated,
One of them we behold.
LEAR
288 This is a dull sight. Are you not Kent?
KENT
289 Your servant Kent; where is your servant Caius?
LEAR
290 He's a good fellow, I can tell you that.
He'll strike, and quickly too. He's dead and rotten.
KENT
No, my good lord; I am the very man.
LEAR
293 I'll see that straight.
KENT
294 That from your first of difference and decay
295 Have followed your sad steps.
LEAR   You are welcome hither.
KENT
296 Nor no man else. All's cheerless, dark, and deadly.

Lear doesn't make the connection. (Kent)

---

282 *falchion* small sword   284 *crosses spoil* vexations weaken   286 *loved and hated* first loved, then hated (Lear and a hypothetical other? Lear and Cordelia? Lear and Kent, who are looking at each other?)   288 *dull sight* dismal spectacle   289 *Caius* (obviously Kent's alias; but the name appears nowhere else in the play)   293 *I'll . . . straight* I'll attend to it shortly   294 *difference and decay* quarrel and decline   295 *You . . . hither* (Lear fails to make the connection)   296 *Nor . . . else* i.e., no one is welcome here

Your eldest daughters have fordone themselves,   297
And desperately are dead.   298
LEAR   Ay, so I think.
ALBANY
He knows not what he says; and vain is it
That we present us to him.   300
EDGAR   Very bootless.
> *Enter a Messenger.*
MESSENGER
Edmund is dead, my lord.
ALBANY   That's but a trifle here.
You lords and noble friends, know our intent.
What comfort to this great decay may come   304
Shall be applied. For us, we will resign,
During the life of this old majesty,
To him our absolute power; *[To Edgar and Kent]* you to
   your rights,
With boot and such addition as your honors   308
Have more than merited. All friends shall taste
The wages of their virtue, and all foes   *310*
The cup of their deservings. – O, see, see!
LEAR   *Cordelia*
And my poor fool is hanged: no, no, no life?   312
Why should a dog, a horse, a rat, have life,
And thou no breath at all? Thou'lt come no more,
Never, never, never, never, never.
Pray you undo this button. Thank you, sir.
Do you see this? Look on her! Look, her lips,
Look there, look there –   *dies still diluted,*
> *He dies.*   *still blind*
EDGAR   He faints. My lord, my lord –

---

297 *fordone* killed   **298** *desperately* in despair   **300** *bootless* pointless   **304**
decay ruin, Lear   **308** *boot* reward; *addition* advancement in rank   **312** *fool*
a term of endearment; here, Cordelia (the fool disappears after III.6)

KENT
Break, heart, I prithee break!
EDGAR   Look up, my lord.
KENT
320   Vex not his ghost. O, let him pass! He hates him
321   That would upon the rack of this tough world
     <u>Stretch him out longer</u>.
EDGAR   *space*   He is gone indeed.
KENT
     The wonder is he hath endured so long;
     He but usurped his life.
ALBANY
     Bear them from hence. Our present business
     Is general woe.
       [To Kent and Edgar] Friends of my soul, you twain
327   Rule in this realm, and the gored state sustain.
KENT
     I have a journey, sir, shortly to go.
     My master calls me; I must not say no.
EDGAR
330   The <u>weight</u> of this sad time we must obey,
     Speak what we feel, not what we ought to say.
     <u>The oldest hath borne most; we that are young</u>
     <u>Shall never see so much, nor live so long.</u>
                   Exeunt with a dead march.

Edgar ends the play.

---

320 *ghost* spirit   **321** *rack* a torture instrument   **327** *gored* wounded

The distinguished Pelican Shakespeare series, newly revised to be the premier choice for students, professors, and general readers well into the 21st century

All's Well That Ends Well
ISBN 0-14-071460-X

Antony and Cleopatra
ISBN 0-14-071452-9

As You Like It
ISBN 0-14-071471-5

The Comedy of Errors
ISBN 0-14-071474-X

Coriolanus
ISBN 0-14-071473-1

Cymbeline
ISBN 0-14-071472-3

Hamlet
ISBN 0-14-071454-5

Henry IV, Part I
ISBN 0-14-071456-1

Henry IV, Part 2
ISBN 0-14-071457-X

Henry V
ISBN 0-14-071458-8

Henry VI, Part 1
ISBN 0-14-071465-0

Henry VI, Part 2
ISBN 0-14-071466-9

Henry VI, Part 3
ISBN 0-14-071467-7

Henry VIII
ISBN 0-14-071475-8

Julius Caesar
ISBN 0-14-071468-5

King John
ISBN 0-14-071459-6

King Lear
ISBN 0-14-071476-6

King Lear
(The Quarto and Folio Texts)
ISBN 0-14-071490-1

Love's Labor's Lost
ISBN 0-14-071477-4

Macbeth
ISBN 0-14-071478-2

FOR THE BEST IN PAPERBACKS, LOOK FOR THE

Measure for Measure
ISBN 0-14-071479-0

The Merchant of Venice
ISBN 0-14-071462-6

The Merry Wives of Windsor
ISBN 0-14-071464-2

A Midsummer Night's Dream
ISBN 0-14-071455-3

Much Ado About Nothing
ISBN 0-14-071480-4

The Narrative Poems
ISBN 0-14-071481-2

Othello
ISBN 0-14-071463-4

Pericles
ISBN 0-14-071469-3

Richard II
ISBN 0-14-071482-0

Richard III
ISBN 0-14-071483-9

Romeo and Juliet
ISBN 0-14-071484-7

The Sonnets
ISBN 0-14-071453-7

The Taming of the Shrew
ISBN 0-14-071451-0

The Tempest
ISBN 0-14-071485-5

Timon of Athens
ISBN 0-14-071487-1

Titus Andronicus
ISBN 0-14-071491-X

Troilus and Cressida
ISBN 0-14-071486-3

Twelfth Night
ISBN 0-14-071489-8

The Two Gentlemen of Verona
ISBN 0-14-071461-8

The Winter's Tale
ISBN 0-14-071488-X

FOR THE BEST IN PAPERBACKS, LOOK FOR THE

In every corner of the world, on every subject under the sun, Penguin represents quality and variety—the very best in publishing today.

For complete information about books available from Penguin—including Penguin Classics, Penguin Compass, and Puffins—and how to order them, write to us at the appropriate address below. Please note that for copyright reasons the selection of books varies from country to country.

In the United States: Please write to *Penguin Group (USA), P.O. Box 12289 Dept. B, Newark, New Jersey 07101-5289* or call 1-800-788-6262.

In the United Kingdom: Please write to *Dept. EP, Penguin Books Ltd, Bath Road, Harmondsworth, West Drayton, Middlesex UB7 0DA.*

In Canada: Please write to *Penguin Books Canada Ltd, 10 Alcorn Avenue, Suite 300, Toronto, Ontario M4V 3B2.*

In Australia: Please write to *Penguin Books Australia Ltd, P.O. Box 257, Ringwood, Victoria 3134.*

In New Zealand: Please write to *Penguin Books (NZ) Ltd, Private Bag 102902, North Shore Mail Centre, Auckland 10.*

In India: Please write to *Penguin Books India Pvt Ltd, 11 Panchsheel Shopping Centre, Panchsheel Park, New Delhi 110 017.*

In the Netherlands: Please write to *Penguin Books Netherlands bv, Postbus 3507, NL-1001 AH Amsterdam.*

In Germany: Please write to *Penguin Books Deutschland GmbH, Metzlerstrasse 26, 60594 Frankfurt am Main.*

In Spain: Please write to *Penguin Books S. A., Bravo Murillo 19, 1° B, 28015 Madrid.*

In Italy: Please write to *Penguin Italia s.r.l., Via Benedetto Croce 2, 20094 Corsico, Milano.*

In France: Please write to *Penguin France, Le Carré Wilson, 62 rue Benjamin Baillaud, 31500 Toulouse.*

In Japan: Please write to *Penguin Books Japan Ltd, Kaneko Building, 2-3-25 Koraku, Bunkyo-Ku, Tokyo 112.*

In South Africa: Please write to *Penguin Books South Africa (Pty) Ltd, Private Bag X14, Parkview, 2122 Johannesburg.*